all my truths & one lie
fabiola francisco

Dear reader,

This magical town of Glastonbury inspired this story & its deep meaning. I wanted to leave a copy here to share the story.

Happy reading & enjoy!

XO,
Fabiola

books by
fabiola francisco

Standalone

All My Truths & One Lie

Perfectly Imperfect

Red Lights, Black Hearts

Twisted in You

Memories of Us

Restoring Series

Restoring Us (Complete Series)

Resisting You (Aiden and Stacy Novella)

Sweet on You Series

Sweet on Wilde

Whiskey Nights

Rebel Desire Series

Lovin' on You

Love You Through It

All of You

dedication

To the wild girl, who lost her way and found it again. Love is a truth. Forgiveness is a strength.

author's
note

I wrote this story pulling a lot of myself and my experiences, blending them with a love story that is deep. Through my recent years, I've spent time becoming more familiar with spirituality, how energy works, and the importance of healing our emotional pain.

Years ago I began working on myself and realizing my own self-worth. It's been a rocky road, like any healing process. However, it's been so liberating to understand why I carry certain beliefs.

Through my personal and professional trainings, I learned how our ancestors impact us in the present. Something I never paid much attention to before. I learned that we carry loyalties tied to those ancestors that affect us. It has shifted my understanding and perspective and also encouraged me to heal, knowing I am capable of such strength.

I feel honored to have been able to combine my love for fiction and my passion for guiding people through their healing to write a story I believe in so much.

All My Truths & One Lie takes you on a journey about the weight of family secrets, the effect of traumas, and how meeting someone so magical in a mundane world can stir it all up so you can finally look at yourself and become free of the baggage. So you can believe you are worthy of love.

Navia is a reflection of me, and because of that I've been afraid of publishing this novel. I do feel like I have a message to share, and I hope you connect to a part, or all, of it.

I thank you for taking the time to read this book, and I hope that by the end of it, you have also had the chance to understand that your past doesn't have to control your present. Mostly, I hope you have the courage to live authentically, proud of who you are and the road that led you here.

Love,

Fabiola

prologue
dim stars & faded dreams

When I was a little girl, I used to wander around the playground and contemplate life. I didn't understand some things and understood others way too much. I processed information differently, in a weird way, and I didn't understand why my friends were so . . . immature. Yes, at the ripe age of ten, I wondered why kids acted like kids as if I had some wisdom they didn't have. It wasn't that I did, I just saw things differently.

I had friends, but I distanced myself. I needed to as a form of regaining my sanity, or center, or . . . I don't know. Simply needing some time. Too in my own head, that's what I was told. I was too serious. Too reserved. Too wild. A plethora of adjectives that didn't always mesh, yet completed me. I couldn't argue with those descriptions, I knew they were true. A girl who fantasized too much, warred with the desire of a fantasy and the need to accept life wasn't that.

And then I grew up.

But nothing changed.

I stare up into the sky and sigh. My eyes close for the briefest moment as the warm breeze kisses my skin. Sitting in the dark, wondering why I live in a place that outshines the stars, the artificial lights illuminating the insincerity that swirls around this city. I open my eyes to see one twinkling star. It brightens and dims as I look at it, wondering how far away it is and what it's called.

I push my body back to sit straighter in my chair and cover my face with my hands. *How long do I have to stay here for?* I keep telling myself I stay in the city because I still have lessons to learn from it. Maybe I need to stop judging it so much so that I may move on. Lord only knows.

I check the time on my phone. I'm nowhere near tired, but if I don't sleep now, I'll be exhausted tomorrow when my alarm clock goes off at six-thirty. Five hours of sleep isn't nearly enough for me to function anymore.

I glance up at the sky one more time and blow out air through my mouth. *Soon.* I feel it in my soul.

The last three years have been a pause in my life. I've discovered things about myself, grown internally, but the life I led has stopped. Almost as if I needed reclusion to overcome a hump. But that causes distance between myself and the world around me. The more I traveled within, the more I secluded myself. I can say it's symbolic to Jesus's forty days and forty nights in the desert. However, I'm no Jesus, and this seclusion didn't ground me. Instead, it uprooted me, yet my body wouldn't move forward.

At first, I looked at that time as temporary. Then it became permanent. My perception of it became obsessive to the idea that I'd never move from it. Until I realized the peace in the moment. I removed veils of illusion and took the pause for what it was—a preparation for what's to come.

I feel the pull in my soul, guiding me like the wind against a sail. I can allow the guidance or resist it and risk experiencing the greatest shipwreck of my history.

I choose to listen. I decide to go where the pull takes me when I've spent many nights staring at the sky like tonight, telling myself I wasn't ready.

I am.

So many times, the tug I feel is familiar. Another soul

calling to me, awakening this intense need from its slumbering state, just enough to rouse me. Then, it releases, not quite prepared for the intensity of our union, yet a consciousness of each other's existence. It's a building fire I stoke, gently allowing the flicker to intensify.

But I miss him.

I don't know him physically, and I miss him. My soul longs to be near his. In my sleep, I long to feel his arms around my body, his breath tickling my neck. I can sense him inside me. How can you miss someone you haven't yet met?

Homesick for a person my eyes haven't seen, but my soul is familiar with. We've danced together before in other times and I long to see him again. Hold him. Feel him near.

And I'm finally ready.

That's why I took this first step in the direction I want my life to go.

Seeing as my mind is racing and my eyes are wide open, I stay outside in hopes I'll catch a miraculous shooting star. The street light shines on the outside of my home. It's small but cozy. This is what I need for now. As long as I have a chair, a small table, and open skies, I'm happy.

Despite having this home, I still feel stuck. As if my soul is moving faster than my body. I see things shifting in my mind's eye but don't see the shift in my life around me. Or maybe I do. Sometimes it's difficult to see the change when those around you are blind to it. But on the inside . . . on the inside, I feel as if my cells are shaking to a vibration that I'm unaware of. As if something inside of me wants to shake itself free and go at a speed I've never experienced in my life.

Hence, my inability to rest.

A surge of energy bursts, fueling my mind to think

beyond the world I live in. I always have to take a minute to breathe and ground myself. It's easy just to allow my mind to float to a world that many don't believe in. It's natural to see things with a different understanding. And it's so difficult to bond with people because of this. So many times I keep quiet, leaving my ideas to myself in quiet observation. A few times I express what I'm holding, usually resulting in odd looks or silent disapproval.

I shake off the feeling of not belonging and go back to admiring the stars. I can't see the moon from here, but I know she's out there. Another reason I wished I lived somewhere with less light and population. A forest in the middle of nowhere with traces of ancient civilizations and history so deep, it trespasses my bones and hits my soul.

A place like that exists. I just need to find it.

This is why you struggle to make friends.

I roll my eyes and ignore the side of me that is rational. I've learned to embrace who I am. I've learned I may never meet anyone in their thirties who will share the inquisitive wonder I do. I've learned that there's more to life than egotistical existence and material gains.

But those have been easy lessons in comparison to the ones that tore me apart like an angry tiger and then sewed me back together like a gentle horse.

1
finally

I run my fingertips over the pink velvet petals of the flowers that line the garden path. The early morning dew transfers onto my fingers as I trace the sage-colored leaves. I stare up, squinting my eyes before closing them all together. The sun rays paint a smile on my face. Behind my eyelids, I collect tears of gratitude like I collect used books.

It has taken me some time to get here, but here I am, in the place I was born to be in. Here I am living my *purpose*.

I wrap my coat around me as a shiver travels through me. Spring has just begun, and the mornings are chillier than I'm accustomed to. I look back at the unfamiliar flower. The inside of the petals has a darker shade of lines that design them like the chaotic highways I left behind.

No.

Nothing here screams chaos like the angry words I left behind from strangers insulting each other because their egos controlled their hearts.

In this place, hearts outshine egos. The energy that swirls around the stone walls penetrates even the toughest rock. I wipe my cheek and move on to another flower while the birds sing a song of joy above my head.

I haven't been living here for long, and on the first day, the fear that used to rule me tried to cripple my will. But I remained firm in what I knew was right for me and faced the self-doubt like a goddess instead of a victim. One look at the late night sky reminded me that I didn't leave behind anything of value. Instead, this change added value to my existence. What I left was part of the journey that always meant to lead me here.

I check the time on my watch when I notice the sun is higher in the sky and leave behind the flowers that I enjoy daily. I inhale the scent of fireplaces burning around me. A reminder that it is still my favorite time of year. Fortunately, the rain has subsided a bit this week, allowing me to take my time as I walk to work.

Work.

I don't even consider it work. When you are living your passion, the term "work" becomes irrelevant.

Stopping at a crosswalk, I undo the buttons of my coat and allow the chill to cool me from the walk. On the ground, I see a small white feather. Grinning, I squat and pick it up. There was a time I would cringe at the idea of holding a feather, but now I see them as signs from the universe that I'm on track. A way for the angels to speak to me.

I pocket the feather in my coat and cross the street that leads to the office. Some days I question how this became my life. What did I do to deserve it? Then, that same day, I'll have a client that comes to me with lack of self-worth, and I find myself guiding her and myself out of the hole of doubt and worthlessness into the light of self-love.

One of my ongoing lessons—I'm worthy. Worthy of life, love, abundance, prosperity.

Living in a world that easily disregards our value if we're not pretty enough, skinny enough, fashionable, it's easy to forget that worth comes from a place beyond the material dimension of this earth.

I agreed to no longer live in the density that weighs me down and drowns me into a sea of judgment, anger, and resentment. That no longer has a place in my life, if I choose to move forward with a life I've always dreamed of.

It's time I no longer hide behind a veil of pretending and own who I am, show the world the magic within me and all around us instead of hiding for fear of being unaccepted. Truth is, people will judge you regardless. It's in our nature as humans to do so. Therefore, I've decided to step into the light, remove masks and limitations that cause us to blend in when we should all truly stand out for our own individuality.

"Good morning, Navia."

I smile and pull the feather from my pocket before removing my coat and hanging it on the hook by the door. I move further into the room where Makenna is sitting on the couch, stirring her tea. I place the feather in the white, ceramic bowl on the side table housing all the other feathers I have found on my way here.

"Morning," I smile and sit on the chair opposite her. She eyes the bowl and shakes her head. "They don't disturb you."

"They don't." She sets her tea on the table and pauses, smiling at my quirk.

I've only known Makenna for a short time, but I can read her, and I'm aware when she's at ease and when she's overwhelmed. When we met in the small café, I was fascinated by her approach to life. And her accent, I've always been fond of the accent.

We talked for a few hours, realizing we both had similar interests and experiences. My usually guarded stance was immediately removed when the older woman smiled and threw out a British joke I didn't understand.

What I thought was a mindless decision on her part turned out to be a real offer—work with her where she provides holistic services. I agreed to start the next day, showing up at work and realizing it's everything I ever dreamed of for myself. A place full of balanced energy, woodsy incense, and pale walls, I've been using it as my office since then.

"Are you excited about today?"

I nod. "I am. A bit nervous, too, but I'm ready."

"You are." Makenna smiles, the wrinkles framing her eyes a sign of wisdom. "How's the book coming along?"

I shrug. "Slowly." *The book.*

"Patience. Remember, slow and steady wins the race. This isn't like anything else you've written before. Be easy on yourself and allow the creativity and wisdom to flow."

"I am," I smirk. I was up late last night working on just that. After meditating, I took to my laptop to allow the inspiration to move through me. I know this book is different than those I've published before, and I am aware that being here will also open those gates that have been begging to be flung wide so I can burst through them.

"At what time does your first client arrive?" Makenna breaks my thoughts. I check the time on my phone.

"In fifteen minutes." I leap from my seat and rush to my small office. It's perfect—cozy and warm. I light the pine candle on the wooden, hexagon side table and play the "Gayatri Mantra" from my laptop. Taking a few moments to center myself, I close my eyes and inhale deeply before exhaling to the same count. My breathing soothes me.

I then grab the file with my client's name and prepare for her arrival. It's been a few years since I became a certified life coach, yet I continued to put it aside. Something was missing. Now, I am complete. With a variety of tools to truly help guide people, I can offer them the best I have.

As soon as I hear voices in the small entrance, I step out to greet my client. Leading her into the office, I work with her on releasing judgment and realizing her worth.

༄

"You did great today," Makenna smiles as she locks the door behind her. "This modality will be a great tool."

"Thanks. It did turn out great. And a lot more people came than I expected." I smile and widen my eyes.

When I mentioned to Makenna that I wanted to offer a group session to guide people in reaching the root of their personal challenges and limitations, she rapidly agreed and encouraged me. We organized it all in one week, and the last thing I expected was to have over twelve people show up.

I walk into the crisp evening and watch as the sun sinks in the distance. I pause and look around. The town is active, and my heart flutters at the scene of people walking about.

Lifting my bag onto my shoulder, I make a right and decide to write in a small pub instead of at home. A change in scenery will be good for my inspiration. I hope.

Dim lighting and sweet aroma wrap me up as I walk into the pub. I'd trade writing at Starbucks for a place like this any day. I sit with my laptop opened, skipping the beer choices and ordering a coffee, determined to focus. Bringing my phone to life, I open to the image I'm using for this chapter.

My eyes close and I feel the breeze of the day swooshing over my skin and the tie I feel to a place like that. Peace and gratitude. It was then that I made the final decision to make a change. The image reflects so much light and serenity, exactly what I need to inspire this book.

I begin typing and deleting. I sip my coffee, blowing the rising steam from the mug. I type again. More deleting.

I sigh and stare at the picture. *What did I feel there?* As if an image would communicate a message to me. I inhale and exhale expectations, my mind is overworking this project. Let it be that I decide to *finally* do this after the months and years of waiting, and I freak.

Self-sabotage at its finest, ladies and gentlemen.

I roll my eyes at my own obnoxious thoughts and look away from the screen. Too much pressure. Too many expectations when it comes to this book. I need to release it all.

Pretending it's journaling just for myself, I slowly begin writing. Memories of the Celtic site provide a comforting mood as I close my eyes and type what I recall.

I blink a few times to regain focus. Looking from my empty cup to the people around me, I'm jolted to a stop. A warm smile and eyes find me and my heartbeat kicks into overdrive. I tilt my head, gazing at the familiarity in him.

If I told my friends this, they'd all think I've lost my mind. That's partly the reason I keep things to myself. It's also why I am no longer friends with half the people I used to be.

Blue Eyes is now amused, and I realize I've been staring at him while trailing off into my mind. I offer a tight-lipped smile and look down.

"Hi." A deep voice pulls my gaze up.

I smile. "Hi."

He takes a seat without asking and leans forward on the table. "I'm Matthias."

"I'm Navia," I reply. "Nice meeting you."

"Lovely to meet you. American, huh?" I nod. "What brought you across the pond to our town?"

"Adventure," I shrug. *And you,* I keep this to myself. I wonder if he feels it, too—the tug that pulls us, the invisible chord that has bonded us since the beginning. *I'm crazy. What if this isn't him?*

I look into the smiling eyes and sigh. *It must be.*

"Adventure," he repeats, tossing the idea around.

"What kind of adventure?"

"A change in scenery and energy. Something that would take me closer to my purpose in life."

"Has it worked?"

I nod. "So far." I close my laptop.

"Were you working?"

"Kinda. No real progress, though."

He tilts his head and looks at me, a smile sneaking up on his face. "Maybe you need the proper motivation."

I smirk and nod.

We both turn our heads when we hear his name being called.

"Sorry about that. My mates are pissed already. We're celebrating James' birthday. The blond." He points to one of the men.

"Drunk, right?"

Matthias cocks an eyebrow and smirks. "Familiar with British talk?"

"Not much. I lived in Spain a few years back and worked with British English in a secondary school. Learned a thing or two. Mostly, I have an infatuation with the accent."

"Whereabout in Spain?"

"Leon. North of Madrid."

"I know of it. Spain is beautiful."

I nod. "I love it. My family is from there."

"And you chose to live in gloomy England instead?"

"Winter in Spain is gloomy, too. Northwest. This reminds me of it."

When they call out his name again, he shakes his head and looks at me. "I better get back and make sure they don't cause any trouble. Can I borrow your mobile?"

I scrunch my eyebrows but hand it over.

"Great. I've just sent myself a message. Now you've got my number, and I've got yours. I'll be calling you, Navia," he promises with a gleam in his eyes.

"Okay." I look up at him, a calming sense washing over me.

"Very soon."

I watch him return to his friends, one of them slurring something about me and open my laptop again.

Matthias.

His blue eyes are a beautiful contrast to his dark hair. I feel a familiar tug, a knowingness in my core of another time with the same eyes.

I knew he'd be here. Or someone like him. I didn't have a name or face, but I had a feeling. I had a soul connection to him. Seeing him, meeting him, stirs so much.

I sound crazy.

But I know it's the truth. A truth many don't understand or believe in, but we're all tied to another person, beyond soulmates. The invisible cord that weaves our past and present.

With renewed inspiration, I type the words I'd held captive for too long.

2
unwanted truths

Something inside me guided me to move here. It was a voice telling me where to go, and for the first time in my life, I listened. I put aside plans and what-ifs and left. It's the closest thing to throwing a dart at a map, something I've always wanted to do. And I did it with courage instead of fear, when fear so often has ruled my heart.

I inhale the cool morning air and lean on the railing. I look down from my small balcony at the quiet morning in this town. Chirping sounds from a nearby tree in the garden housing my apartment building. Staring at the shapes the clouds make, my mind wanders to Matthias.

What if he was just flirting for the fun of it? Or untrustworthy?

I don't know many people here and with my excitement of meeting him, it's easy to mix up true feelings with illusion.

I shake my head and focus on the singsong of the birds.

I'm a runner. Not in the physical sense of the word, but in the emotional. I ran when I was five when my favorite person died. I ran when I was eight and was touched inappropriately. I ran the first time a man told me he loved me.

It's my defense mechanism, like so many others.

I run when things get hard, and I run when they get easy. I get bored and look away, or I shut down and become numb to feelings.

I'm tired of running. Emotional sprints are more exhausting than physical ones, and I'm tired of the years of reversal I need to do to cut the ties from it.

So, no more running. I look down at my chest. *No more running*, I whisper to my heart.

I walk back inside, grab my phone from the couch where I threw it, and head into the kitchen to make tea. As the kettle heats, I unlock my phone and stare at the message again. I bite down my smile until I remove my teeth and allow myself to *feel*. I want to feel the excitement and happiness. I want to be free to enjoy this. Thoughts of an ending locked away in the back of my mind.

It doesn't have to end.

I reply to Matthias, letting him know I'll be free this weekend.

Six words shook me with nerves and anticipation when I read them this morning. *When can I see you again?*

I can't help but wonder if he felt the familiarity I did. Or if I'm the crazy one that thinks we're connected by souls before bodies.

I know nothing about him except for what my mind conjured about the next man I would meet. I'm scared that his reality is not what my expectations are made of. But I've learned expectations are nearly a push of the ego in the opposite direction of our heart.

His response is quick, and I smile upon reading it.

Matthias: is today the weekend?
Me: not exactly
Matthias: guess I'll have to spend the next 3 days getting to know you via mobile

Matthias and I send messages throughout the day until my phone rings in the evening. Butterflies flap inside my chest when I see his name and answer. We talk about a lot of things, mainly my purpose for moving here. He has questions that I struggle to answer. He wants honesty and, though I feel like I can give him that, his direct approach causes hesitation. Self-doubt creeps in like the constant buzzing in my ear. What if he isn't the person I imagined? What if he doesn't understand? What if I allowed my excitement of meeting someone with beautiful eyes and a gentle smile to convince me it would be this easy?

I'm more careful throughout the rest of our conversation, and he notices. After we hang up, I close my eyes and take a deep breath.

I'm moving forward, not backwards.

I used to be a wild child. Fearless. Brave. At what point did I stop being wild? At what point did I allow society to condition me? At what point did I start giving a fuck?

Unfortunately, I remember what it was that caused the wild girl to become silent and hide, instead of shining bright. I wish I were her today, though, as I get ready to meet Matthias for a date. It's helped that we've spoken each day, but the nerves are trying to take over.

I used to think falling in love was for fools. I used to think people believed it to be an irresistible necessity that would blindly control them. I saw it as a weakness to allow another person to influence my emotions. People were weak and hungry for it. For someone else to tell them how to feel, someone else to accept them because they couldn't accept themselves. It was a mirror I never wanted to look at because I was the one not accepting myself. It's not that I believed love was for the weak, it was that I was too weak to feel it. Too afraid to hand another person the opportunity to reject me the way I rejected myself.

I've left myself heartbroken as much as the men in my

life have. Maybe more. I've lost count.

It all started at such a young age. When you've been betrayed, touched, marked by people you trust, it shakes you. It creates a depth that makes you question how life can be that way. It skins you, leaving you exposed. Easily shattered. It leaves you caged to the shame, wondering if everyone could read it on your skin. So, I created a barrier that would lose my truth and live the lies of how I wished my life would be.

Sometimes I wish my heart hadn't learned to love. Some days it's easier to stay closed and hard, black and bitter like the coffee I love drinking. But I was intrigued to feel it. I was curious about what it would feel like to be enchanted by the magic of love. I found out it was poison instead.

I was born into a corrupt family, and the more I learn how deep that corruption ran, the less I remember the good of those who came before me. Their foul actions repulse me when I reach into my being and uncover the truths that were hidden from me. The less I love. The less I can forgive. The more I believe any kind of love is full of false promises. A fun game people enjoy playing because they're masochists. Those games leave me breathless.

This is why I began releasing what I could. I tried to shed it all. Sometimes, though, the self-loathing is nonstop. I wear a cloak of shame so no one can see what I'm trying to hide. Instead of shedding, I cover up. It's not easy to let people see who you are so openly. I've been re-teaching myself that experiences guide us on a path, leading us to where we need to be, making us live through things that we need to so we can evolve.

"So, you're saying that we carry over loyalties through our DNA from our ancestors?" Matthias leans forward, his chin resting on his hand.

"Yes."

"I could be carrying bullshit from some old geezer I never met?"

I try to decipher if he's teasing or serious. I don't talk to people about this unless I know they share the common knowledge, but Matthias kept digging deeper, for more than superficial information, like how many siblings I have. He asked the right questions to lead to this point in our conversation, and I'm wishing he hadn't. At least not on our first date.

Better to be transparent from the beginning.

I nod in response and take a gulp of water from my glass. Matthias didn't question my water order instead of an alcoholic beverage. I'm glad he got a beer instead of feeling as if he had to stick to water, too.

"What about karma then? We also create our own," he states.

One side of my lips lift in a small smirk. "We do, from previous lives. That doesn't take away what we carry from our ancestors. We belong to the same soul family, whether our father is our father in this life and our sister in a past one. The souls all belong to a unit. So we carry from them, and we carry from us."

"That's bloody awful. I have a lot more work to do than I thought."

I exhale and lean back on the chair. The smell of Indian spices surrounds us in the small restaurant. When he asked if I liked Indian food, I eagerly nodded.

"Do you believe in past lives and that kinda stuff?"

"Do you see where I live? It's a mystical town in the middle of England. It's embedded in us."

I laugh and nod. "That's what attracted me to this

town. The openness to the magic of the universe, and not in a trendy, new-agey kinda way."

Matthias nods, pensive. "Have you trekked up to Glastonbury Tor yet?"

"No. Makenna said it's better to wait for when the weather warms up a bit more."

Matthias shrugs. "With the proper coat, it's not too bad. I'll take you there, next time."

My head leans back and my eyebrows rise. Matthias chuckles. "Yeah, there'll be a next time. We're just getting started, Navia." His grin is wide and honest, the kind that puts you at ease with a simple glance.

Don't sabotage this.

I barely nod.

"You know that the hill was a labyrinth. Well, it still is, but you can't really follow the track."

"I didn't know that. I only know its connection to King Arthur and Avalon. And not much at that."

"We're definitely going there. And Glastonbury Abbey. I'll need more than a few hours in the evening." He sips his drink.

"Okay."

"Are you finished?" He nods toward my plate.

"Yeah."

"Great. I'll pay, and we'll go for a walk." He smiles that charming smile again. The one that captured me from across a pub five days ago.

I see women in my life go head over heels for a man, change their lives, only do things that will please them, and I don't want to become like that. While I want a loving relationship that is a balance of giving and taking, I do believe that it goes both ways. I don't want to become a woman who stops her life because of a man, whether he asks for it or not, and takes shit from him when she doesn't need to. I want a man who will treat me with respect and love I witness women easily doing things for men when they won't even do it for themselves.

I vowed to break that pattern, from my family, friends, society. That vow has built a wall though. A guard where I give off the vibe that I don't need anyone. It's made me hard. And sometimes, I want to be soft. I want to be okay with allowing myself to give my all to a man. The balance of give and take got distorted, still creating an imbalance—instead of giving and giving, I take and take.

I don't want to do that with Matthias. I want harmony, and to have the kind of relationship that I finally know can exist between two people. I want a balanced partnership between two beings.

So, when he grabs my hand as we walk out of the restaurant, I don't shake it loose. When his light-hearted laugh moves through me, I don't allow it to bounce off a stone wall that rivals those in this town. I bring myself to the present, to the reason I'm here. I remind myself I no longer have to live in doubt. I'm free of those limiting ties.

Matthias tells me about growing up in a place like this. We talk more about what I do for a living, and I mention the book I'm working on.

"Why are you blocked?"

I shake my head. "I don't know. I have all the ideas in my mind, I just can't seem to ground them onto my laptop."

"You said you've published before?" I hear the question in his voice.

"Yes. Mostly romance novels."

"And that's easier to write than this?" His curiosity is painted in the lines on his face. We've stopped walking and are now standing on the sidewalk in the middle of town, hands still holding.

"Yes. It's fiction," I state matter-of-factly.

"And fiction is easier to write?" he still asks.

"Of course. I make up stories, I write lies about difficult relationships that find perfect endings. Everything is forgivable in fiction."

His eyes narrow, scrutinizing me. "And not everything is capable of forgiveness in real life?"

I simply shrug.

"Isn't this what you do with your clients? Guide them in finding forgiveness, among other things?"

"Yeah." I realize how contradictory my statement is.

"Tell me, why can't we forgive in real life what we're capable of forgiving in made up stories?"

"Because fictional hearts are more compassionate than real ones." Even I hear the uncertainty in my words. The question I'm begging him to answer.

"You write compassion into your characters, so you must believe the characters are redeemable. If they can forgive, then you must pull that from inside of you. A part of you that also forgives."

"I used to think so." How did we get to this? He asked about my book, why did I lead the conversation down a jagged path of buried hatred?

As if sensing my discomfort, he smiles. "You're capable of forgiveness, Navia. You'll get this book done, and I'm sure it will be a great success."

We begin walking again in silence, the chill in the night sky cooling me from the heat burning in my center. I gaze up at the sky and, although this town isn't as isolated as the middle of a mountain, I see twinkling stars dancing in the black paint streaked across the sky.

I've always wanted to live in the sky, with the stars as

my neighbors. Sometimes I forget that I do live on this earthly plane. That the things I want to grasp are millions of miles away, in a different world. And tonight's conversation is a sure reminder that I'm firmly rooted to this planet.

Sometimes living is too heavy.

When I shiver, Matthias tugs my arm until I'm close to him and swings his arm around my shoulder. This may be the first night we go out, but it feels like home.

3
confessions

I've had it all and lost it all. I've been on top of the world and face down in the dirt. What I've never had was average, the things that normal people know.

I'm extreme in a world where mediocrity rules. I don't know a middle ground. I'm all in or all out, but I can't be somewhat invested. I pretend to be, for the world, but internally I'm warring with myself for being a hypocrite.

So, when I love, I love hard or not at all. There are no likes or maybes. My heart knows right away when something is right. Sometimes I don't listen to it, just to experience something other than huge excitement or major regret. In reality, I still feel the same. We can't change who we are, even when we pretend to be something different than we were born into.

My dad gets me. My mom struggles. I've learned not to blame her anymore. She's a result of the equation she was brought up in—prim, proper, lock away the secrets and forget you own the key. My brother is like her—rational, analytical, methodical.

I'm a moon lover and sun admirer. A night owl and early riser. I love them both. I hate the middle of the day. It drags. But living in dawn and dusk fuels me to move through the rest of the day with some energy. My father and I are the same, I think. I've never asked him, but when I was little, we'd stare up at the sky and search for the man on the moon. I wrote that into a book once. It was a tribute to him, to the person who gets me completely, who doesn't judge me for being a bit reckless and a lot harsh.

The cursor on my laptop taunts me. The words I told Matthias yesterday about writing coming back into my thoughts like a court jester, teasing. Maybe I can take a trip back to Spain soon. I can return to the place that inspired this. It could help.

I sigh and drop my head on the table, my forehead slamming the fake wood harder than I meant to.

My mind has been on Matthias all day. I romanticize the idea of relationships, despite my hard exterior, measuring them to this perception I have in my mind of what they should be, who people should be in them, and who they shouldn't be. It's why I write romance. In fiction, I can allow those illusions to flow freely.

I'm an observer by nature, constantly taking in my surroundings even when I seem to be disconnected. I can't disconnect. I can't turn off my nature. So I watch people— their expressions, their form of communication, body language, emotions. Sometimes I wish I could stop for a minute, take a break from the constant pull of others. It's the cure and curse of being an empath. The ability to help humanity that I have seeped so deep in my soul is there, but sometimes humanity is a heavier load than I can carry. Sometimes my heart snaps at the idea of others suffering. Sometimes I'm the one suffering when I'm expected to be the healer.

So, I choose to stay alone. It's easier than the disappointing realization that love will never be what my imagination has come up with. Exclusion over disappointment. But what if, just once, I shatter every preconceived notion I have and live? What if, one time, I cross a stranger, we exchange a look, and a memory of

31

another time unfolds behind both of our eyes? A spark of something deeper than observed human interaction and comparisons. He'll look me in the eye, and I'll look at him, and we'll both *remember* who we used to be with each other.

Maybe.

Maybe that's my romanticization approach to all that will never be. And that is my truth.

But with Matthias, I felt that deep connection. Fear that it's all part of my wild imagination instead of a reality shakes me. It won't be the first time I confused reality for the craving of a made-up truth.

I lift my head and stand. I pace around my small apartment until I go to the balcony and look out onto the darkened town. Everyone is sleeping. I assume so at least that at three-thirty in the morning on a Sunday, well technically Monday, that the town is resting for the new work week.

I should sleep, too. I have a full schedule tomorrow, including a private session on the new modality I did with the group last week. I know that kind of process can go way beyond an hour, and I need to be present, not focusing on the past I meant to leave behind.

There comes a time in your life when you must come face to face with your ghosts, or they'll forever haunt you.

I'd be lying if I said my ghosts haven't been lurking lately. During the day, when I see the beauty of this place, I swim in the joy of having broken away from the bungee rope that kept holding me back. But still, I have things that are starting to resurface. Feelings demanding my attention, things that I don't want to deal with. I thought I was free from them, but like I told Matthias, forgiving in real life isn't as easy as writing pretty words on paper and ending stories with a happy ending that usually makes me want to puke.

The pressure in my chest I've been ignoring bangs against my ribs again. I roll my shoulders in, bringing them into myself.

A deep breath.

Then, two.

Five deep breaths.

The pain is still reminding me that if I don't forgive, it will only hurt me. The others are already six feet under.

"Let's go for tea." I snap my head to the right to look at Makenna.

"You scared me."

"You did seem a bit distracted." The wrinkles around her eyes deepen as she scrutinizes me.

Stiffly, I remain still and wait for her to finish looking at me. "Tea," she repeats with firm authority.

I finish putting the crystals away and grab my bag, following her out of the office. We walk in silence the short distance to the café where I first met Makenna. The afternoon sky is gray with heaviness swirling around us as it threatens to unleash a raging storm on us. The wind picks up as we duck into our destination.

The neutral tones and the smell of coffee and spices calm me. I know Makenna well enough to know that this isn't just a tea break in our day.

"How was your weekend?" she starts.

"Good." I scan the menu so I can avoid her eyes, though we both know I'll order chai tea.

"Did you write?"

"A little."

"So, you stayed home the entire time?" She's fishing for me to open up.

"No," I draw out. "I went out. On a date," I exhale.

"A date?" I laugh at the view of her eyebrows shooting up.

"Yes." I drop the menu onto the table.

"That's wonderful. How did you meet?" She leans in, ready for my story.

"I met him last week at a pub." For some reason, I want to keep this to myself. I trust Makenna, but Matthias is still new, and I don't want to make a fuss about this.

"Good for you." She leans back and sips the tea she ordered. "You did seem a little lost in your head today. If you need to talk about anything else, I'm a great listener."

"Well, you're a therapist, so I assume you are." She cringes at my use of therapist and I chuckle. I know how much she hates being called that.

"Cheeky girl," she smiles.

"I'm okay. Processing some stuff. You know how it is." I ease her mind, knowing she'll worry something is wrong with me. I've been off today, the talk about forgiveness stirring sleeping ghosts.

"Well, dear, if you feel you want someone to simply talk with, I can be a neutral party." Her hand squeezes the top of mine, comforting.

"I appreciate that."

"Now, tell me about this man you met. What's his name?"

I roll my eyes and smile. I figured she'd keep asking about him. I tell her how we met and what I felt, feeling a bit embarrassed to admit my initial reaction. I sound like a naïve girl when I hear myself say that I think Matthias and I are connected from long ago. It's so cheesy, but deep down, removing the front of hating romance, I do believe in soul connections.

"I'm glad to see you making friends instead of hiding

behind that laptop, driving yourself bonkers. The book will get written when it's time. You can't force inspiration, or it won't be the truthful wisdom you're meant to share."

I nod silently.

"You know," she looks up at the ceiling, three fingers loosely over her thin lips. "There was a time I resisted all of this, rebelled. I didn't want to believe in anything or anyone. No god or angel or saint. I couldn't believe there were higher powers that would allow the darkness in the world to take over. Why would we have the power to hurt each other so greatly?" Her rhetorical question is hanging in the air with the steam of tea.

Her eyes find mine, and I tilt them downward.

"I never really understood the power of free will and why we have it. Not if it was meant to be used for pain. I never understood why there was evil until I took a class that went into detail on yin and yang, polarities, balance, and how we *all* have light and shadow. You could imagine my stubborn mind refused to believe I could carry shadow like those I judged.

"I guess the reason this old hag is telling you this is because I learned that this three-dimensional experience is a choice we make. We chose to return to this place with the baggage we carry to heal our soul. The universe is so complex, yet so simple. Forgive yourself and free your heart, the rest of the world will fall into place."

I stare at her, unblinking. I know exactly what it's like to feel that way, to doubt the good because of all the bad that exists. But just like Makenna, I've also learned the reasoning behind this experience we all call life. It's not about the destination, but the journey. In this physical world, we all end in the same destination—dead. It's how we get to our death that counts. It's the steps we take and the opportunities we grasp to better ourselves and heal that will determine how we lived our journey.

Sometimes, though, we're just not ready.

Sometimes I sit completely still, staring at a wall, calming my overactive mind. I freeze, a pause in time and the world stops spinning for a while. It's what I do when I have too much on my mind.

It's what I'm doing now, as I remember Makenna's words from this afternoon. I reflect on them, allowing them to resonate with me because I too have been down that path.

When I moved here, when the pieces started falling into place, I thought I was done with a lot of the bullshit I was carrying. I felt free. I felt free before I stepped foot on this land, before I made the final decision to come live here. And I was free, in a sense, because I was healing pieces of me. What I had ignored is that we heal in parts. We deal with what we can handle in that time in our life, process it, and grow from it. But that doesn't mean we're done.

I thought I was done.

There are things we carry that are so deep in our soul, it takes more than meditation and ho'oponopono to someone's soul to clear the hurt. Some marks dig deeper than others, and I've discovered I'm carrying some that have excavated to the depths of my soul.

Therefore, staring at a wall in total silence brings the peace I need at times, shifting my focus from density back to a path of forgiveness.

Many times, I've been told forgiveness is the key to our personal happiness and freedom. The person we need to forgive doesn't even know it at times, it doesn't affect them. It eats us up, though. The hatred is like maggots eating away at decaying flesh.

Growing up, and even as an adult, it was difficult for me to mesh with peers. I think it's because I was carrying so many things I didn't know how to process, and I felt displaced. I've always felt displaced—with my family, friends, in different jobs. Most times, I felt like an outsider looking into a nucleus that I was never invited to join. I now think it was my own energy giving off that feeling. I was blocking myself so much from others seeing me and learning my truths, that I excluded myself. I used my barrier so they could only see the glimpses I would offer, keeping the rest so tightly locked because I was ashamed of it.

I was raised to keep the secrets inside our house. Whatever my parents told us, was always between the four of us. Whatever we were dealing with, no one else had to know.

Trust no one.

I took it to heart. I inhaled that belief stronger than an addict inhales cocaine during a relapse. I swallowed it and placed it around my heart. Trust was too valuable to gift out freely, and I was taught we couldn't trust people openly.

Words have vibrations, and those vibrations are embedded in us. I took that mantra and laid my life's blueprints around it.

It's been a motherfucker to break that belief and accept that trust isn't a weakness.

Now that I've met Matthias, I'm more determined to break it so I can have a real shot with someone I'm connected to.

Matthias.

He called, but I didn't answer. I wasn't done staring at the wall. I wasn't done drowning knowledge I wish I never learned.

But secrets are gravediggers if kept hidden.

And I don't want a grave, I want to be cremated.

I shake my head and blink my eyes. I'm so morbid at times.

My phone lights up, luring my eyes to it like a mesmerizing mermaid singing underwater.

I stand and walk to it, knowing it's a message from Matthias before I see his name on my screen. I read the words and smile, responding to him. We've talked every day, allowing our connection to grow whether we've seen each other physically or not.

My phone vibrates again.

Matthias: can I ring u?

I smile and tell him yes. Waiting for his call, I stare at the phone like a psychopath, so you'd think I wouldn't startle when it actually started vibrating in my hand.

"Hello?" I sit back on the sagging couch cushions.

"Hi." His deep voice travels into my ear and lands on the overactive part of my brain that's been warring with my heart lately. "How was your day?"

"Good, and yours?" I tilt my head back onto the back of the couch and close my eyes. "I just realized I don't know what you do for a living," I blurt out.

"I work in IT. Software, analytics, boring stuff."

I can hear a smile in his voice. "I doubt that."

"I actually love what I do, but to anyone else it's rubbish. Too many details and explanations that are complicated. Anyway, I was wondering if you're free tomorrow for dinner."

"Um, yeah, I think so," I fumble over my words.

"You think so?" His accent deepens with his amusement at my reaction.

"Yeah, I'm free. I finish work at five."

"Bloody marvelous." I hear him shifting, wondering if he's lying in bed as he talks to me. Wanting to get more comfortable, I make my way to my room, shutting off the lights on the way, and lie on my side.

Matthias and I talk for hours about life and our beliefs in certain situations, like the power of meditation and past lives. It feels weird to talk about certain topics without a second thought with someone I just met. Some topics aren't for everyone, and I protect them and myself.

With Matthias, he immediately jumped in, asking the questions I couldn't refuse to answer. It's as if he gets what rattles my passion and pokes it awake. From what we've talked about, it's clear he has knowledge of the spiritual world, and not just because he was born and raised here, in this mystic town. However, we still haven't talked about people having loved in other lifetimes, and the draw souls have because that would be too much, too soon, for me to admit.

I'm not a trusting person. I struggle. I open myself, willing to allow people to enter, but those triggers return in a sweeping moment. Instead of knocking down, they rebuild layers of stone that I had worked on chipping away. Suddenly, I'm back to the beginning. Back to the start of everything, and I scold myself for allowing these shots to penetrate my soul. It takes time to allow someone in and milliseconds for that door to close, locking out everyone.

I'm not a trusting person, but I want to be, for him and for me.

Matthias is someone who deserves a fair chance. And I deserve someone willing to win over my heart.

The noisy pub rattles me in a welcoming way. People

laugh and talk, drinking beers and eating with friends or family. Some small children run around, ecstatic to be given the freedom to roam while their parents are too busy to reprimand them. I look across the table at Matthias. His eyes are bright, a lighthouse in a black sea full of restless creatures swimming around. The creatures are all in my mind, tapping me for attention—a nuisance I thought I had released, but his eyes fill me with a tranquility that is new to me.

Instinctively, I look away when his gaze becomes too intense, as if he's analyzing the war I'm fighting within.

Trust.

Don't Trust.

He's different.

They're all the same.

If one of the people you admired and trusted the most was a monster, then any stranger can hurt you.

I'm so deep in my head, I'm ruining our night. I'm caged in the dollhouse of my mind, walls painted pretty to hide the pain I'm holding.

What caused this? I was doing well.

"Is this always so full on a Tuesday?" I ask Matthias, hoping the conversation will stop the onslaught of questioning in my head.

"Not always. The children started Easter holiday today."

"Easter?" I hadn't realized that was coming up so soon.

"The town will be busy with spring activities and people happy about being on holiday."

"I'm sure it's a lot of fun."

"Are you having fun now?" He raises his eyebrows.

"I am."

"You've been lost in your mind most of dinner. If you want to go home, we can."

We.

Infinite memories we have yet to create cross my mind like an endless loop. I see myself with him, living.

"Do you want to go for a walk?" I ask.

"Let's." His confidence soothes me.

As we stroll through the dimly lit garden surrounding my apartment, I inhale the chilly air and fill my lungs with freshness.

"This garden was all I needed to see when deciding to rent my apartment. I saw it, even in the dull, early spring weather, and felt its beauty. I'm so glad this is where I chose to live." The meaning is double, because moving to England was the best choice I could've made for myself.

"It's a beautiful area. You're close to the centre as well."

"Yeah," I sigh. I take a seat on a bench. Matthias mimics me and remains silent. I keep my eyes trained on the shadows ahead of me. "Do you believe souls are destined to meet when they incarnate as humans?" I finally turn to look at him.

His eyes are trained on me, his face a map to the treasure I've been hunting for. "I've always believed that."

"Me, too," I whisper. "It's partly the reason I came here," I confess. "I knew there would be people here who I'd connect with. That sounds crazy, huh?" I throw it out as a joke.

Matthias's cool hand finds mine before he speaks. "Not at all. Sometimes, in my dreams, I'd see a woman, the feeling of being with her, it's indescribable. At least on a physical level. I think we make soul agreements to cross paths before we're born."

"I've had dreams like that, too. I always thought it was my soul connecting with his through a subconscious state.

That's not something I could say to just anyone so openly."

"I get it." He gives my hand a gentle squeeze, and when I look into his eyes, I see the same recognition I feel reflected back at me.

Bravely, I ask, "Do you know who the woman is?"

"Yes." One word escapes his breath before the same lips land on mine in a slow reunion.

My arms reach around his neck. My body moves closer to him. My eyes flutter closed. And my heart, it roars to life.

Goosebumps break out on my skin like a love-fool's epidemic. Our tongues dance to a song our souls orchestrated long ago.

If I ever had a doubt about the significance of meeting Matthias, it melts away at this moment, when I feel the pulsing of his energy mixing with mine. One energy. One soul.

The thought freezes me. I abruptly break the kiss and watch Matthias's narrowed eyes and heaving chest stare at me with confusion.

"Holy shit," I whisper.

"I know."

My heart is sprinting, threatening to run me off my course. I knew he was important, but . . . did I know it'd be something like this?

Twin flames.

"Are you ready for this?" His body relaxes.

"I think so."

"You have to be sure."

My fingers skim his face and brush away the longer strands of hair that are covering his eyes. "It won't be easy."

"No," he shakes his head.

"No wonder so many things have been surfacing since I met you."

"For me, too, but it's part of our path," he shrugs.

"What if…" I look away and shake my head. "Never mind, I don't want to call that upon myself."

"What if you ruin it?" My head turns to him with creased brows. "If we met, we were destined to. No coincidence I saw you at the pub drinking coffee while working, no less," he chuckles.

"I thought you were a soul mate," I reveal.

"So much more."

I've learned about this, heard stories in workshops I've taken and read about it in articles I've stumbled upon. I knew Matthias would be here, in this place, when I moved. What I didn't know was the depth of our connection. Or maybe, deep in my soul, I did, and fear blocked it.

This isn't going to be pretty, yet it's going to be amazing. *Yin and yang.*

4
baggage

When I was a little girl, I used to wish I was a vampire. The idea of having to feed off of blood was what stopped me from thinking about those things. I didn't want all that, but I wanted to live an immortal life. I would've done anything for immortality. I'm convinced my mind wasn't that of a normal child. Then again, the things I lived probably triggered me to want the kind of strength those vampires had. I wanted to be stronger than the humans that threatened those who couldn't defend themselves.

Instead, I lived in a city where people would turn into some kind of zombie and eat human flesh while high on some kind of drug.

I swear, I try not to laugh, but I can't help the dry chuckle that escapes at the ridiculousness of it all. Then, I wonder why those people would take that drug. How would they feel when they sobered up and realized they ate part of their mom's arm? I shiver. At first, I didn't believe it, and I'm glad that trend ended quickly.

Anyway, back to my original thought. *What was it again?*

I lean back on the couch and look around my small apartment. It was already furnished when I rented it, so it's been hard to add my own touch to it. I squint my eyes as the fading sun trespasses through my window. I came here to live in a place full of forests and magic, fairies and peace.

Why am I stuck in the past? *Because it is tangled with the present.* The past brought me here. It shaped me to make the decision to move, to fight, to surrender. It was rough growing up with the idea of a perfect family, only to be stripped of that idea when I was an adult. I still need to find forgiveness and doing it away from the constant physical reminder was necessary. The pressure in my chest is still too great when I think about everything that's happened.

I've written about some level of forgiveness in all my novels, allowing the characters to grow through their journey, yet I'm still rooted, unable to forgive. Actually, I think each day I hate more. I resent more. Lately, anyway.

My chest tightens even more. The war inside destroying my peace like an uncontrollable wildfire that takes with it a person's entire security.

Why would Matthias want to be with someone like me? Just a tiny glimpse into the thoughts that swirl around in my head is enough to scare even the bravest person. I am not delicate lace. I'm wrinkled, tattered, linen that's frayed. And I can't disguise myself anymore.

No more veils.

No more masks.

No more pretending.

My eyes trail around the room again, wondering what it would be like to share this space with someone like Matthias. We just met and I'm already getting in over my head. But now I know that this will happen too fast with him. I'll fall because our tie goes deeper than the love we know. We are woven together, life after life, since the beginning of our essence, and now we're both here, physically.

I used to want a cowboy that loved the simple life and owned a red barn. While I'd still love that life, I now know that it's more than that. It's more than the illusion I served myself to fill the silent vacancy of my heart.

I know why I wanted that life, but I'm not ready to

admit it out loud. Some things are still too difficult to process, too fucked up. The truth is ugly when we take the time to dissect it. I'm not ready to be so forthcoming with myself, let alone with the world, and I'm certainly not ready to tell you all the twisted things I carry.

Both heels of my hands press against my chest. I gasp for air, needing to fill my lungs, devouring air, before I lose it and destroy the life I'm trying to build.

You're crazy.

I woke up with the thought of immortal vampires as a result of last night's date. Since I don't have clients today, I figured I'd write. Three cups of coffee and one tea later, and I'm still sitting on the couch, no words written, thinking about blood-sucking creatures.

And imagining living with Matthias.

I cover my face with my hands. My relationship with Matthias won't be like anything else I've experienced. It will be powerful, challenging, and unstoppable.

My eyes find the small tattoo on the inside of my wrist. A daisy. When I was little, and all was right in the world, I used to love picking the small, white daisies people call weeds. They were beautiful, adding color and life to the pale green grass.

Wildflowers. Just like me. Wild and rebellious, like the weeds that grow where they're not wanted.

I'd pluck them and hold them, wishing they'd live forever. The irony isn't lost on me now as an adult.

That's one of my favorite childhood memories. At least I think it's a memory. I've learned that a lot that I believed was real was actually illusions painted in my mind. Maybe that's the trick your brain plays when trying to make you forget about the truth you live, the trauma.

Except I never forgot. I always remembered and buried

it deep into my psyche.

I didn't want to deal.

How could you? How could you want to resurface the confusion, fear, and shame?

So I remembered flowers, white and yellow, that I used to pluck petals out of, asking if he loved me or loved me not. Who *he* was is still unknown. It was just fun to tear them apart the way I had been. I didn't see it then, but I see it now.

We're all a product of our environment. Patterns repeat. We carry on what we choose to own from the older generations. I don't get why. To heal, I'm told, but I have enough to heal to add this burden.

Release.

I take a deep breath and look at the screen. Maybe this is what I should be writing. Instead of enlightened words about the universe and our purpose, I should write the pain that led me here. The disappointment. The anger.

Back to flowers.

I close my eyes and breathe in the humidity that surrounds me as if I'm back to seven and innocent. Maybe this will help clear the fog. I know others like me who forgot. In blocking the abuse, they blocked the light. Only carrying an odd weight, they couldn't understand where it came from. But it was there. Except, I was a product of someone else's abuse.

Maybe it started before then. I don't know. When I was five, I swore my paternal grandfather in Spain got a small bird for me after I spent all summer begging for one. He died that fall. I returned that winter. The bird was in a cage. We let it go after my grandmother showed me.

Apparently, that was all a lie. The beautiful memory I have was torn to shreds when I asked my mom about it, and she told me that never happened. I was thirty then, realizing my mind had conjured some beautiful fantasy.

Maybe this is just how I deal with trauma. Illusions.

Or maybe *she* forgot because her own memory needs to be blocked.

So many maybes. I want certainties.

Back to flowers.

I've never spoken to anyone about the abuse. I swallowed it, knowing no one would understand. I was wrong. I wasn't the only one. Patterns repeat themselves. Why haven't we healed them?

But I needed to protect them. I wouldn't be responsible for destroying a life, a family. So I buried it like people want to bury the weeds they refuse to see beauty in.

Because what I know now is that the person who was abusing me, was being abused. It's warped when you learn love means to touch and be touched against your will.

That's why I don't believe in love, at least not in the archaic sense of the word. Love is nothing but manipulation, a way for both men and women to abuse power. A way to lie.

Men aren't worse than women. We're all bad. Humanity has been deranged for years, bringing forth pain instead of compassion.

But we're growing. We're evolving.

That's what I'm supposed to be writing about. Our evolution, our growth. The way we connect with our souls and the light we feel beyond the physical. Yet, I continue to be drawn to the dark. The shadow. The part of us that keeps us on this plane, this dense dimension.

Maybe it's time I spoke my truth instead.

The weight of that thought knocks me down. I can't. What if someone reads it? What if they figure out the truth and blame me? Or call me insane, dramatic, a shit talker wanting to stir the damn pot when it's harmoniously simmering?

I carry these secrets, and I'm tired of it. I can't bear to hear people praise men and women who don't deserve it.

Don't judge.

I roll my eyes and exhale. I know we all come into this world for a specific role, and I accept that. Some of us are victims, others, perpetrators. I cringe using the word victim, but it's a reality. Whether we own the vibration of the word or not is up to us. But when it's in your family, the judgment comes in stronger. Suddenly I'm playing God and deciding who can be forgiven and who can't.

Then I remember where we come from. The stardust my soul was born in. *I chose this.* I don't understand why. Did my soul need to experience this to ascend? Is this the test of ultimate forgiveness?

That must be it.

And I can't forgive the person who started it all. At least in my eyes, he did because maybe this started generations before him. Maybe he was the pioneer. The Saint in Red.

I know he's not the only one to blame, but I've gotten my claws hooked on punishing his soul.

My god, I need help.

I shut the laptop down and look around. All of this because of one tattoo. What will come when I look at the rest of them and nitpick?

I throw on some clothes and slip on my shoes before heading down, sans laptop, and finding a place to eat and get some more coffee. I grab my raincoat before taking the stairs down to the street.

I cross a few smiling people as my legs burn with the

incline as I walk on toward the town center. Eyeing a crystal shop, I make a note to stop by after I've eaten.

The gray clouds above soothe me as I take my time arriving at the café. The thoughts that are drowning my peace wash away with the light drizzle escaping the clouds. In the distance, I see Glastonbury Tor, and I think of Matthias's suggestion of going there. If he's on holiday, maybe we can go. Unless he has plans with his family or friends. I don't know much about his life, even though I know his soul. It's a weird revelation.

Finding the café, I walk in and sit. Anything connected to King Arthur and I'm hooked. I found this place after living here for only a few days and read the name, and I knew it would be a favorite of mine.

After I eat, I cross the street to St. John the Baptist's church in search of the one thing that will help ground me. I see the labyrinth on the grass and smirk. Taking a few deep breaths, I begin walking the winding path, mind clear.

When I first found this labyrinth, I stared at it for a long time before I walked it. It grounded me then, and I'm hoping it will ground me now.

Peace begins to settle into the pores of my bones. My heart slows. I keep my balance as I arrive at the center of it, swaying a bit as I go. I pause, closing my eyes, tilting my head back a bit so the soft drops land on my face.

Hearing voices nearby, I open my eyes and begin my return to the opening of the labyrinth.

Weightless, I make my way back to the street that leads to the crystal shop. These stones are my savior. I have plenty, but you can never have too many gems gifted from earth.

"Hi," I tell the woman behind a counter as I enter, admiring the shimmering colors. I immediately walk to the amethyst, my favorite of all. I stare at the pointed peaks and deep purple before moving on to another crystal.

I wonder which one helps aid forgiveness.

"If you need help, please let me know," the woman smiles.

"Thank you."

"You're the new woman working with Makenna, aren't you?" She tilts her head.

"I am."

"That's wonderful. I had a few people come in talking about your class." The woman rounds the counter.

"Really? That's awesome," I smile. I gained a few new clients from my workshop. People who wanted to dig deeper and work through their emotions, releasing emotional baggage that isn't theirs.

"You're new to the area, right?"

"Yeah. From the States. In case the accent wasn't obvious," I joke.

She laughs lightly. "I'm Ada. Are you looking for something in particular?"

"I'm Navia," I offer. "Do you have pink quartz?"

"Of course." I follow her to a glass case holding different crystals. "Take your pick." She leaves me to it, returning to her spot behind the counter.

I look at the few pink crystals, feeling their energy before picking the one that resonates with me.

"Beautiful," Ada says when I reach the counter to pay. "It will fill you with compassion," she winks.

"Thanks," I say, shifting and avoiding her eyes. *Am I that obvious?*

With my new crystal in a bag, I find a park and sit on the damp ground. I remove it and hold it, feeling the coolness on my palms as I close my eyes to allow its power to take me away, or bring me home. The people talking and the children playing is background music for my meditation. I slowly begin to release tension, relaxing as I focus on my breath. Inhale. Exhale.

I am a being of light. I repeat my inner mantra. The same one that always allows me to believe I'll survive an airplane flight.

With swirls of colors behind my eyelids, I give in to my meditation until a portrait invades the beautiful colors, staining them with anger. I squeeze the quartz, its rough edges marking the skin on my palms.

I hate him.

I hate him.

I hate him.

The peace of light has been replaced with resentment as the person's face zooms in and out of my mind's eye. Stubborn tears build behind my closed eyes, but I refuse to let them fall. Squeezing my eyes tighter, I take a deep breath. The pain in my chest is back, but the face of the man won't leave me alone. I know I need to work through this. Move through it. I just don't want to. Clenching my jaws and giving the crystal one last strangle my eyes spring open. I toss my head back as my heart slows its pace in the racetrack that is my chest.

When I refocus on the park, I see a pair of blue eyes watching me. I see him across the concrete path that divides us, and he smiles. I remain seated as I watch him approach me.

Without a word, he sits next to me, places the crystal on the ground, and pulls me into a hug.

I let him.

For the first time in years, I allow another person to comfort me.

"Let's go."

"Where?" I look up at him from the comfort of his chest.

"Trust me." He leans down and kisses my lips, chastely.

"Are you up for a walk?" he asks as we step on the street bordering the park, his hand holding mine.

"Sure."

His free hand cradles my face, his thumb brushing my pink cheek. I feel as if the particles inside my body are pulsing erratically. His lips graze my forehead. "Let's go on an adventure."

I smile, feeling the anger from earlier slowly leaving me. I need to work through it, but right now I don't want the past and the ghosts of the dead to haunt the present moment and my time with Matthias.

"Where are we going?" The scent of rain floats in the wind as he guides us down the road, away from the center. "Are we going to the Tor?" My eyes widen.

"Seems fitting for a day like today. Wouldn't you agree?"

"Thank you for showing up."

He shakes his head. "I saw you sitting there, eyes filled with some kind of memory. I didn't want to interrupt you. Not until you were ready."

"I had a dream last night, or early this morning. It shifted my entire mood. I thought if I'd go for a walk and have breakfast, I'd feel better. It was working until I tried to meditate with the quartz. Emotions I've buried are fighting to be released. They're fighting for my attention."

"Give it to them, give them the attention. Feel it and let it go," he advises.

"It's not that easy," I whisper.

Matthias stops walking and faces me. "I know it's not,

but you're strong. You chose this path because you're capable of walking it."

He tugs my hand and begins walking again. I know he's right, but my mind is trained to punish by not forgiving. Realistically, that's only hurting me.

The closer we get to the Tor, the more visible the tower becomes, like a powerful giant standing above the town, watching.

I watch as Matthias guides us with certainty. "How often have you come?"

"Thousands of times. It's where I go when I need to disconnect."

"It's your happy place," I confirm. Matthias nods. "I have a place like that in Spain. Celtic homes. Well, what's left of them. The site brings me inexplicable peace. It puts my life into perspective. It gives me a purpose."

"Is that what you're writing the book about?"

"Yes, except lately I'm questioning if that's what I *should* be writing it about," I confess.

"What do you mean?"

I stop and look at him. "Maybe I'm going about the purpose of the message all wrong. Maybe the message isn't supposed to be about reaching enlightenment, but about shadows we face on the path to enlightenment. Because really, if we were all enlightened, we wouldn't be on Earth."

Matthias chuckles. "Forget expectations. Forget the idea you had for this book. Write what you're feeling. Write the truth." He places his hand over my heart.

My breath catches on an inhale. We're now at the base of the hill, but my attention is all on him. "What if the truth hurts the people I care about?"

"Holding the truth for yourself will hurt you."

I blink back tears and nod. *The truth.*

"Let's climb," he demands. We begin to ascend up the stone path that leads to the tower above. The mystical Isle of Avalon, as it's believed to be.

I stop mid-climb to take in the view, admiring the town below, and catch my breath. I take out my phone and snap a picture of what's below and of the emerging tower above. Matthias waits with a gentle smile as I look around. We've been quiet on the climb, each of us sorting through our thoughts.

He was right, this is helping my mood and state of mind. I continue to walk, the *baa* of a couple of sheep a few feet below putting a smile on my face.

As soon as we hit the top, I pause and admire the stonework of the only standing tower left from the past. I slowly turn, taking in the panoramic view.

"On a clear day, the view extends miles all around."

"It's gorgeous." The wind swooshes around me at this altitude. I walk into the tower, feeling the rough stone chilling my hand and look up at the opening above. I allow my body to feel the calm sensation as I walk out of the other side and stare at the view, misty from the weather.

"The view of the sky at night must be incredible. Have you ever come at night?" I turn to look at Matthias, staring at me.

"It's beautiful. On a clear night when you can see the stars."

"I can just imagine. There is nothing more peaceful than stargazing. It's one of the things I missed in Miami. The stars are limited to a few specks in the half-lit sky because of all the lights."

"I'm glad you moved here." He grabs my hand and stands next to me, looking out at the world spread out before us.

"I am, too. I knew I'd meet you here," I confess on a silent whisper. His head turns to look at me. "I just didn't realize how deep the connection would be. I could imagine, but this isn't something you can concretely make up in your mind." I blink back tears that well in my eyes. Matthias gives my hand a squeeze as he takes in my secret.

My heart pounds in my chest, knowing I have emotional baggage to clear and release if I want our relationship to withstand time. He doesn't speak. Instead, he leans down, his lips brushing against mine, his hands holding my face close to his. I grip the back of his shirt, pulling him closer to me, as he swallows my doubts.

5
expectations

"Let's take the other path down to get that view as well," Matthias suggests once we're ready to head down from the top of the Tor. "How do you feel?"

How do I feel? Good. Confused. Angry. Which answer do I give him? I don't want to hide from this anymore. I morphed into something I wasn't long ago to deal with my experiences. To numb the obvious truth that I'm not like the people who were in my life. I always felt misplaced, misguided. I was holding so much inside, protecting others, but no one was protecting me. *Where do I belong?*

I belong with myself, accepting myself. Until I do, I'll continue to float in a world that is strange and judgmental, because the reflection I'm receiving is that of my own.

I go for honesty. "I'm not sure how I feel. Up here, in this space, I feel peace. Emotions have been surfacing. Well, you saw how well I'm dealing with that when you spotted me meditating."

"It's all part of life. We get hurt. We dwell in pain. We take action to release it. We heal. We learn. We grow. It feels like bloody torture at times, but if we resist it, it will only deepen the scar."

"I know."

"For a long time, I wanted nothing to do with spirituality. My family has always been open and free when it comes to beliefs. We aren't religious, but we believe in a higher power, God, Allah, use the name you like. When I was younger, I rebelled. I wanted nothing to do with it because I couldn't accept that something so divine would allow people to act like savages.

"I stopped going around my parents' house for a while. I did everything in my power to exclude myself. I turned to technology, science. Things I could work out and experiment with a concrete result. Science gave me evidence and proof that spirituality did not. It also made me face everything I was avoiding." I'm enthralled in his story.

"How?" My wide eyes stare at him.

"Someone who had hurt me when I was a child reached out to me to help him with the computer system he used for his business. I turned him down, but it pierced through me. All the reminders."

I step closer, hugging him. Silent tears drip down my face as I hold him to me. He runs a hand down my back, soothing me when it should be the other way. I look up at him.

"Do you ever let someone comfort you?"

His throat bobs as he swallows. "I'm not used to it."

"Me either. It's weird to let someone else take care of you. Let me comfort you now, though. I want to." His patterns on my back stop, both hands holding on to me as he buries his face in the crook of my neck. I brush my fingers through the ends of his hair on the back of his head, the slight curls there rolling between my fingers.

Soft lips peck at the base of my neck before dark blue eyes search my face. "Thank you," he whispers.

I move my fingers over his face and smile. "You're welcome."

"Do you want to have lunch?"

"Yeah." We continue our trek down the giant hill and back into town.

"Tell me about the book now." Matthias leans back on his chair, both of our plates empty.

"I started with an idea I had. The process came to me one day, to use the photographs I took the last time I was in Spain. Hear what the pictures were saying. I thought it was insane, but figured I had nothing to lose when it came to seeking inspiration."

"And they haven't inspired you?" He purses his lips.

"Somewhat. Mostly, I stare at them and then at my document. I know expectations kill us, but I had expectations for this book. Writing romance is much easier for me."

"Why?" he insists.

"We've talked about this. It's easier for me to make up pretty stories with just enough pain that the characters can overcome. Real life isn't as simple as a linear plot with one climax to overcome. Glastonbury Tor reminded me of a plot's formula. You start at the base and begin to climb, pausing to live and breathe your surroundings. It's a bit of a struggle, the incline. It's new and takes a bit of adjustment. Then you reach the top, the unknown. You may feel as if you can fall off the edge of the mountain with the brush of the wind. But you overcome it, walking through the dimness of the tower and out to a new view, a new perspective. You figure out life at the top of the hill, and everything is clear once the fog diminishes. Then, you begin the walk down, much faster and easier, until you reach the bottom of your journey."

Matthias stares at me, his eyebrows slightly creased and the hint of a smirk on his mouth. "Did you just compare the mythical island of Avalon to the plot of a novel?"

"Yes."

"And you struggle to find inspiration for what you're working on?"

"Yes."

"You've just used a blend of fiction and reality to create a metaphor. You've just got to write. Forget the bloody expectations. Let go and write. Forget the pretty stories and write the story you're carrying inside of you. The one you were meant to write." His eyes widen with meaning. I simply nod.

"Sometimes writing too many truths makes my heart heavy, so I write lies." It's a day full of confessions.

"It's time to write truths. You're strong enough to hold the weight of your heart. And I'm right here in case you need help." He squeezes my hand as if I need a physical confirmation of his presence. Maybe I do.

Matthias is right. I've been carrying this story. Maybe people need to know about darkness before they learn about the beauty of the light. If we can't identify our shadow, how can we conquer it?

Maybe reading about my experiences will allow others to open and not feel so lonely in this world. I really don't know, but I can incorporate my wisdom into it. I can still use the photographs.

Most importantly, maybe it will help me finally heal all the scars I've picked myself. For choosing to carry other people's pain. While some are my pain, most aren't. I'm angry at people that didn't directly hurt me, but their actions were a snowball effect that led to my own traumas. I've learned too much about how past generations affect future ones to turn a blind eye and call it a coincidence. Besides, the things I've learned turn my stomach. Some things are unforgivable. Except we're supposed to have the amount of compassion and understanding that can forgive anything. I wish I had that amount of compassion uncovered in my heart. Maybe one day.

Just when we think we've overcome all the bullshit; the universe throws us another layer of the work we have to do. I needed to feel complete to move here, to make a choice. I should've known that once here, more would be uncovered.

Away from my family and influences, I can deal with things the way I need to. Not the way others around me expect me to. Not being the fort of strength people have come to see me as. Here, in this beautiful land with cool weather and gray skies, I am finding my place. I am finding people who serve my purpose. I can connect to a truer part of myself that has always been too shy to expose herself.

In this land full of myths about King Arthur, Avalon, and neolithic energy, I can write my truths without the expectations that I'd keep those secrets for others. I'm loyal to a fault. I'll take anything you want to my grave. But at what expense? At the expense of keeping our family in the same cycle? No. I won't be responsible for another child's pain and disappointment. If I have the power to, I'm breaking the patterns that have held us all hostage. I'm rebuilding the backbone that was hit down with the force of Thor's hammer from the one person who held us all up. He failed us.

The Saint in Red.

I swallow back the bile trying to travel up my throat.

"Breathe," I hear a distant voice and gasp for air through my mouth. "Navia."

My dazed eyes find Matthias's blurry face.

"Inhale again." I do as he says and close my eyes. When they reopen, his face comes into focus.

"Sorry."

"Don't apologize. I lost you for a moment. Are you all

right?" His hand cups my cheek across the table.

I nod. "I think so. Just got lost in some thoughts."

"What do you want to do?"

"Can we walk around town for a bit?" I suggest.

"Of course." He pays for our meals and stands, reaching his hand out to me. I look at it and then up at him. Smiling, I take his hand and walk out into the afternoon rain.

"Do you mind that it's raining?" I ask him.

"Not at all," I smirk, lift the hood of my coat over my head and prepare to feel something else besides the past.

After walking in mostly silence for a long time, we return to my apartment. My feet are begging to be released of the confinement of my shoes. If I could walk barefoot everywhere, I would.

Matthias stands in the middle of the living room, looking around, as I walk to the bookshelf and place my new pink quartz next to my other crystals.

"Are those your books?" Matthias is now beside me, looking at the shelves. I nod as I watch him reach for one, frozen as he opens to a random page and reads to himself. I wait, body tense, as he finishes and looks up at me.

"This doesn't sound much like romance," he states.

"It's the one book that isn't romance. It does have a love story."

"I gathered that." He makes his way to the couch, black and red cover still in hand.

"What are you doing?" my voice rises a bit.

"I'm going to read it."

"Now?"

"Yes. Would you fancy I take it home instead?" I shake my head and stare at him. What will he think? What will run through his mind as he reads the words I penned, the only ones that are closest to my truth.

"Do you want anything to drink?" my voice cracks. "I'm going to make tea."

"Tea would be great. Thank you." He looks up at me briefly, with a smile, before turning the page in the book.

Reading my writing is the only way to get to know the depth of me.

I linger in the kitchen, watching the steam rise from the kettle as the whistling announces it's reached the level of heat I need. I stay hidden in the kitchen as the tea steeps for the appropriate amount of time, not ready to meet Matthias's gaze after reading parts of me. When I can't hide any longer, I take the mugs and honey to the living room and sit next to Matthias.

"I don't know if you like honey or not, so I brought it just in case. Also, do you like milk? I didn't bring any, but I have some in the fridge if you want. I know some people drink their tea with milk. I don't unless it's a chai latte." I'm rambling.

He puts his hand on my knee to still its bouncing. "Honey is perfect. Thank you."

"Okay."

He puts the book face down on the coffee table, keeping it open on the current page he's reading. He waits for me to fix my tea before he adds honey to his and takes a sip. I do the same, the usually comfortable silence now a piercing in my calm.

Reading my mind, he speaks. "This story is good so far. I can read so much of your wisdom in it. Have you ever visited Amsterdam?"

"Yeah. I went a few years ago with my brother and cousins while I was living in Spain. It's beautiful."

"I've never been."

"No?" I automatically assumed Europeans travel all

over Europe.

"I've not, but I'm sure it's beautiful."

"It is. I'd love to go back. Visit it in a different light, if that makes any sense," I share.

"It does. The more we grow, the more we see places with new eyes. A different perspective." I appreciate his understanding.

"We do. It's happened to me. The last time I was in Spain, I understood it differently. I understood myself differently, so I was able to feel the magic of nature. Something I didn't have a lot of in Miami."

"But you have beaches," he points out.

"Our beaches are polluted with tourists. It feels artificial."

He nods, pensive.

"And I'm more of a mountain and forest person anyway," I offer.

"We've got lovely woods to visit not too far away. We can go some time." I nod and eye the book on the table. "Does it bother you I read it?"

"No. I wouldn't have let you if it did. It makes me nervous. I keep questioning if you'll know which parts are fiction, and which parts are not."

"Is any of it fiction in this one?" He tilts his head with a knowing smile.

"The plot," I respond.

"But the feelings are yours," he points out.

"Aren't writers the owners of all the emotions they write as creators of them?"

"I think so. Will you show me the photographs you're using for your current work?"

"Yes." I stand to find my phone and settle back on the couch, opening the images. Bodies touching, I begin to show him all the pictures. A sensation builds like a buzzing over my skin with the feel of his body brushing against mine with the tiniest movement.

We talk about the views, the rocks, and the energy that swirled when I visited this site. Matthias gets it. He doesn't laugh or scrutinize me when I talk about something otherworldly, he adds to it and brings his own insight and thoughts. Talking to Matthias is a luxury I don't have with just anyone I meet. Being this open with someone is something I only ever wished for upon shooting stars.

my body, your hands

My idea of relationships has been jaded for a long time. I never really opened up to anyone completely. Not enough for them to see the real me. I'm a chameleon in a way. I camouflage just like the animal I'm terrified of. Oh, the irony of life. It'd always been easier to merge and transform to be like others than deal with the fall of being myself. How fucked up is that?

I never fully understood who I was in order to make someone else understand. All I knew was that I had weird thoughts at times, a different understanding of the world. I started learning there are other people who view life like me. Those are the people I found and held on to.

Now I know myself, but I didn't always. Before, I was kind of lost and morphing from one person to another, shedding each skin as I transformed. From certain clothes to jewelry, I focused on the superficial. I would stop writing poetry when I met a guy. Never confess the parts of me that were in pain. Instead, I'd smile. A temporary fix to my fissured heart. They couldn't fix what was broken long before.

I talk about them as if there were so many men in my life. There haven't been. Not serious ones at least. One boyfriend was serious, and he was my last real relationship. Many years ago. Yet, we didn't stop when our hearts did. We drove ourselves into a grave of disappointments.

I used to have sex with my ex-boyfriend in a car, hidden

in the shadows of parking lots. We had already broken up, but I wanted any chance to be with him. It was dirty and shameful. I didn't feel good about it afterward, but he held on to my soul, the false pretense that he cared about me. Because why would he still want my body if he didn't want my heart?

Naïve, naïve girl.

I hated myself so much afterward. It was years that I held back. I lost a bit of myself more each time I'd meet him for our secret rendezvous. He's no longer a happy memory of young love. We destroyed that when we used each other for different reasons.

Then there were a few others. I got lost in them. I don't remember their names, just how their bodies felt. They are nameless faces I used to prove that one man didn't control me. He did. For a long time. But I was determined to prove he didn't. I allowed men I didn't care for to bury inside of me in hopes one would make me forget. I ruined friendships over it. Good friendships. Deliberately. It wasn't my best time. Too much alcohol, some drugs, no regard for other people's hearts. I barely cared about my own.

When I used to think of what I'd tell people about myself, about my relationship status, I'd blank. I hated people for asking. What was I supposed to say? I have a fear of commitment that won't allow me to move forward. That I was stuck on my ex-boyfriend for ten years, unable to move on. Giving him everything he wanted of me just to keep a connection. A dying hope that he'd see me again once more as the woman he loved. Then, when I was ready to break the connection, he wouldn't allow me. I trained him that way. He held on in any way, snaking his way into my life, reminding me of how good we were together. A snake. That's what he was. But he wasn't always all bad. And I held on to that idea. It's really not fair to make him the villain in my story. I pushed for it. I pulled him in and held on tight. We were drama induced people, unable to let go of our first love.

I would lie to myself that I was afraid of committing when in reality I was determined to burning myself with the body of a man that tore his heart away from me.

It took years to break away, down to blocking him physically from my life. His phone numbers, messages. I wanted my freedom. I wanted my right to heal myself. I couldn't do that with him because it was always easier to escape in his body than to be happy in my own skin.

The darkness of a car never shone a light on my secrets. His hands could brush away, for a quick second, my confusion.

But when doors opened, and lights shone, I'd feel worse than before, adding a layer of his body to the already growing hatred I had for myself.

The day I finally released him is a day I'll always remember. To no longer feel the need to hide in someone was a freedom I was grateful for. It was time for me to make myself a priority. I knew it wouldn't be easy to begin healing, but I'd take it little by little.

I never wanted to fall into that cycle again, so I stayed away from dating. Only one other man took my time after him, but I never gave him my body. He had to prove he was worthy of it. And he didn't.

I wouldn't allow just anyone's hands to land on my body anymore. This time, I'd make the choice out of love, not out of manipulation to keep a man by my side.

I worry I'll fall into that with Matthias. It's a part of me I'm still working on. The fear of abandonment greater than the fear of losing myself again.

I shut my eyes tightly, shaking away memories. With him, I have a choice. With him, I make the decision.

My stomach contracts. The confusion grows wilder as I try to find a balance between what happened and what I felt in the past. I fell victim to someone else's victimization. He didn't know any better. He was just acting on what was taught to him. We were kids that had fallen into the burning hands of twisted adults.

I bite down my lips and suck in ragged breaths as tears blur my vision of nothing in particular. My body coils in, hiding from the past as if it would lash out and burn me.

We were just kids.

I feel the pain of others more than my own, the pain of those who were truly abused. Yet, the thought of someone's hands on me right now is unwelcome. I need to work through this.

The rain has been pelting the windows all day. I want to get out. This Easter holiday has interrupted my work since everyone is on holiday mode. I've seen Matthias a few times since our trip to the Tor the other day. Today he's with his family, and I am here working through my emotions so I can give us a real chance. No running. No hiding. Just Navia.

The book he was reading is still face down on the table, in case he comes back and wants to continue reading it. I walk to the bookshelf, grabbing the pink quartz and one of my journals. I'll take Matthias's advice and remove expectations and write what I'm holding in.

Sitting on the floor, using the coffee table as a surface to write on, I place the quartz next to me and open the journal to a blank page, adding the date and working book title.

I close my eyes and breathe deeply allowing the words to carry from my heart through my arm into the paper.

✑

My body jolts and I peel my eyes open. My head rests on my arms on the coffee table. The journal under me creating an uncomfortable pillow. I hear the second knock. Lifting my head, I rub my eyes and lick my lips. I check the time on my phone. Six-thirty. I must've fallen asleep at some point while writing. I look at the pages of the journal and see my messy cursive scrawled on the three pages I have written. That's better than what I've written lately on my laptop.

Another knock echoes inside my apartment. I stand, knees cracking and stiff, and stretch my arms over my head. I walk to the door and look through the peephole to find Matthias standing on the other side.

"What are you doing here?" I ask as I open the door.

"I called, but you didn't answer, so I stopped by. I wanted to see you." I open the door wider, allowing him access into my home. "Were you sleeping?" he laughs.

"Yes, why?"

"Your face is creased." He runs a finger down my face where I'm sure lines are marking my skin. Proof from the pages in my journal.

"Come in." I walk in, him closing the door behind us. "I'll be right back." I leave him in the living room and go to the bathroom. I observe the marks on my face and shake my head. I wash my face and brush my teeth, waking myself up.

When I walk back into the living room, Matthias has the book in his hands. I sit next to him, peeking at the page he's on.

"Why did you write her as a prostitute?" he asks.

I move to the side a bit to look at him clearly. "Revenge. It was the only way she felt she could control the other gender. That and self-worth. Or lack thereof. All she felt she was good for was her body. It was all control and manipulation."

He nods. "Were you writing?"

"Yeah. Before I fell asleep. I haven't read what I wrote, but I took your advice to remove my mind and let it all out."

"Good."

"How was lunch with your family?" I shift on the sofa.

"It was nice. The weather could be better."

"I like this kind of weather." I lean back on the couch. Matthias puts the book back down and puts his arm around my shoulder, pulling me close to him.

"Tell me about your family," he whispers into my hair.

My body tenses. "You know about my parents and my brother. He's married and still living in Miami. I have a lot of cousins. I talk to some and not to others unless we're in the same room for family events. Just how life has led us. Some of my family is more conservative and closed-minded. My dad's intuitive, but I think he tries to block it most times. As if he doesn't want to know everything. I get it. I used to be like that. What I don't know can't hurt me. Truth is, everything comes to light eventually. Secrets can only lie dormant for so long." Nothing I'm saying makes sense. It's jumbled facts.

"How about your grandparents?"

"They've all passed. I loved my paternal grandfather. He was my person, but he passed when I was young. I was five, I think. It took a toll on me. I have abandonment issues from not processing his death." I swallow back the emotions bubbling at the base of my throat.

"Someone I worked with not too long ago pointed out that his loss hindered my sense of security and a male figure, despite having a great relationship with my father. It made sense when she said it. Things happened after that. I can see how I could've been left vulnerable without him in my life. I

71

didn't even see him often, as he lived in Spain, but I loved him. He was a hard man, but I'm also a hard person. We understood each other. It's hard to lose someone like that as a young child and not fully understand it."

"It is difficult to lose someone you love," he agrees.

"What about you? Are you grandparents still alive?"

"My maternal grandmother is. She's a strong woman. I'm very close to her. In my thirty-five years, she's the one person who has let me go my way. Let me do what I needed to do," he shares.

"That's good. And your parents?"

"We get along. We didn't always, but we do now." I nod in understanding. "What can I say? I'm a bit of a rebel," he chuckles.

"Me, too." A smile lands on my face, and I place my head on his shoulder. "What's your last name?"

"Taylor," he doesn't hesitate to answer. I can't believe I hadn't asked before.

His energy vibrates with mine as they mingle. My skins pebbles with him near. My soul expands. I feel an unknown sensation, yet Matthias is familiar. He doesn't feel like a stranger I met a few weeks ago. Seeing him in the flesh is like reuniting with a childhood friend that knows all your secrets and loves you anyway. It's like picking up after years of no communication and realizing it's as if no time has passed. What is time in the grand scheme of things? Barriers placed by the human mind to create limitations and deadlines. When it comes to the soul, time is limitless. Time is irrelevant.

His hand runs up and down my arm, causing me to shiver against his side. The contact moves through my entire body, awakening parts I've been too afraid to delve into. How will it feel to have his hands on my body after accepting that I wasn't always touched appropriately? No one has touched me since I've stopped lying to myself.

I tremble internally. Sometimes, I wish I was still lying.

7

stardust lovers

I stand by the entrance of Chalice Well as I wait for Matthias
to arrive. I called him this morning and asked if he wanted to
come with me. It's a nice day, and I wanted to be outdoors.
No restrictions keeping me encased. I want to wander and
breathe in nature. Get my feet soaked on grounding soil.
Live amongst the history that stands as our foundation.
When we see it in person, right up in our faces, it's
mesmerizing. How far we've come as humanity in some
aspects and how much we've regressed in others.

I smile as I see Matthias approaching.

"About time you arrived," I tease.

"Sorry." He tilts his head to kiss me. "Are you ready?"
One of his hands grabs one of mine and his other reaches
for his back pocket. I place my free hand on his forearm.

"I already paid."

"Why?" His lips turn down.

"I wanted to," I shrug.

"Sneaky." He gives my hand a gentle squeeze.

As soon as we walk in, I leave behind the laden
memories that have turned predatory since I met Matthias.
Threatening my sanity but pushing my resolve to heal. One
day I'll look back, and the overbearing weight will seem
minuscule. My strength will be my focus as I realize I can
handle more than I thought. I'll get there, I know that. Right
now, I need to feel this.

We walk on a stone path with plants on either side of

us until we reach the waterfall, the area covered in lush green plants and layered stones. The sound of rushing water fills my ears, and the undercurrent of sadness leaves me for a while as I become present in this space.

"This is beautiful." I look around, a few other people in this section with us.

"Peaceful," Matthias confirms.

We wander around, visiting the different areas. Standing in front of the wellhead, I stare at the wood and iron cover. The space here is small, a built-in circular bench made of stone rounding the wellhead. A few people are sitting around, some silent while others chat quietly.

"What is the meaning of the symbol?" I ask Matthias as we sit on the stone bench. The two overlapping circles must be significant as they're spread throughout here.

"Vesica Piscis. The polarities of the feminine and masculine and perfect creation of our being, which would be the center where both circles unite. It's also a symbol for twin flames."

"Oh." I wasn't expecting that, although I can see the femininity tied to this. "And the stick in the middle."

Matthias smirks. "King Arthur's sword."

"Cool." I look at the symbol as people take photos near it.

That's how the union of two people should be—sacred, like the symbolism of these circles. That is what I want. No more hiding behind meaningless encounters and quivering in the dark of night because I am too consumed by the ugly words I spat at myself.

I've worked too hard to get to this space, where I can breathe in peace and exhale negative thoughts that try to conquer me. For a long time, I've kept to myself. I've been a hermit, taking time for introspection. It's necessary at times.

I need to forgive myself as much as I do others, maybe more.

It's weird. I feel like I don't need to tell Matthias what led me here, about my choices. It's as if, in essence, he knows my flaws and accepts them. He won't pretend to give me a sanctimonious lecture about right and wrong. He has flaws, too. We had rough roads to get here, but we arrived at the same time, which is rare.

For that, I'm grateful.

With him, things are different. I connect to him in a way I've never connected to another human. Of course, the reason for that is what creates this union between us so significant.

Warm lips touch the top of my hand.

"Are you ready to see another part?"

"Yeah." I stand with him and we make our way to another section of Chalice Well. "Don't let go."

"Never." His hand tightens around mine to reassure me.

We sit on cushions on the floor in my living room, using the coffee table as a dining table, and open the containers holding our Indian food. We spent the rest of the day wandering the town, stopping in shops where I bought more crystals to use in my sessions while working with others.

Now, with the moon shining outside, we eat with the television playing in the background.

"I loved this series when I was a boy."

I look at the show playing, unfamiliar to me. "What were you like as a boy?" The curiosity of a young, rebellious Matthias seeps through me. I bet he was mischievous. His chuckle confirms my assumption.

"Terrible. I was definitely the kind of child to push boundaries. My poor mother. I loved to be outdoors, get lost. After a few times, she stopped worrying something had happened to me." He looks down, sadness etched on his face.

"Hey." I reach for his hand under the table. "What happened?" I speak softly.

"She should've worried."

"Matthias," his name is sweet on my lips. He shakes his head. "Come on." I get to my feet, tugging his arm. He's slow to stand.

I guide us out to my balcony. It's colder than I thought and I tuck my hands into the sleeves of my sweater before gripping the ornate, metal railing. Matthias stands behind me, his heat wrapping me up like a wool blanket on a freezing, winter night.

"When I feel off balance, I like to stand under the night sky and stare at the stars. They've always been the one thing to bring me complete peace."

"Thank you." His breath tickles my neck. I lean my head back on his chest, searching for constellations. The sky is so much more visible here, away from big cities. The night is clear enough that the twinkling lights are visible.

Matthias places his hands on either side of me, holding the railing. His body cages me in. The comfort of his proximity makes my heartbeat race. It's a contradiction I don't bother analyzing.

"That's Orion's Belt," I point to the three stars aligned.

"It is." Matthias's voice sounds lighter.

"Are you okay?"

"Yes."

"Are you sure?" I tilt my head back further on his chest until I can see his face, a smile breaking out on my lips.

Matthias laughs. "Positive." He reaches down to kiss my lips. "Thank you."

"The stars always remind me that there's something greater out there than the bullshit we live."

"You're right," he agrees.

"It reminds me that no matter what, I'll return to stardust. When I do, I want to be rid of the baggage."

"They're just challenges we chose so we can evolve."

"Why did I choose certain things?" My voice is a whisper.

"I don't know." I watch him shake his head.

"At least we get to admire the beauty above from here." I look back at the sky.

"You and I were born from the same star," he whispers, his breath tickling my ear. "And we'll return to it once again."

Matthias's arms wrap around my chest, holding me close to him. I close my eyes as his scent surrounds me. *Home.* That's what he feels like. As if all the roads I've been lost on finally led to the destination I didn't even know I was seeking. As if I was never really lost, but simply on a journey to get to this point. Meeting Matthias is more than romance. It's more than being in a relationship. This is something so deep, words can't describe it, and most people don't believe in.

Every worry escapes me as I feel this man's arms hold me. We were split from the same source, sent on different paths that mirrored each other until we were ready to meet again.

My arms curl around his at my chest, lacing our fingers. This is a sensation I want forever. This is someone I can't lose. He deserves for me to be fully present with him. We'll bring things out of each other, but only so we can clear them.

When my body begins to shiver, we go inside and lie on the couch, watching reruns of the shows Matthias used to love. I settle in front of him, his arms never leaving my body as he tells me about the episodes in between yawns, until my eyes close.

My eyes blink open in the dark room. I look around. When did I get to my bedroom? I place my hand over Matthias's arm, still wrapped around me. He must've moved us at some point in the night.

He stayed.

I remain still, as to not wake him, and enjoy the sensation of waking up next to him. My legs tangle with his as his soft breathing fills the silence in the room. I have no idea what time it is, and the closed blinds on the windows won't reveal the exact time as they block out all light.

When my bladder can't take it anymore, I sneak out of bed and make my way to the bathroom. Matthias is still sleeping when I return. This time I lie facing him. His lips are parted, and his wavy hair is covering part of his face. I brush it away and lay my head on his chest. His arm finds my waist again and holds me to him.

My eyes close once more and I sleep until light touching on my arm wakes me. I blink away sleep and stare into blue eyes.

"Morning." I clear my throat.

"Good morning, beautiful."

I smile and hide my face in his chest. He lifts my chin and brings his lips to mine. "No hiding."

"Have you been awake for a long time?"

"A few minutes."

I move closer, hugging his body, and place a kiss on his

chest. Just sleeping with him, feeling safe, is so different than the loneliness I used to feel, as if I was missing out on some grand secret others knew about. Waking up next to Matthias, his arms around me, my legs knotted with his, is definitely a feeling I'm glad to uncover.

My body tingles as he moves his fingers up and down the back of my neck, sneaking into my sweater and moving over my shoulder. He continues the same trail, each time building my awareness of his hands on me.

He's a slow antidote to the venom I've swallowed, and his cure is worth the patience of time.

Our eyes remain locked as his fingers graze my skin. I reach the edge of his hair on his neck and run my fingers through it. I used to think I was wasting time by not finding the person I am meant to love for the rest of my life, that I'd meet him too late and miss out on so much. I stopped searching after a while, knowing the pressure would only push him further away. However, the small fear that I'd meet him too late would creep up. I wanted to feel him all around me as soon as possible, so we'd have years to love one another.

Now that I've met Matthias, I realize that what I feel is so much stronger than I could've imagined. It takes away the mentality of limited time because suddenly I understand what people mean when they say love is limitless.

Love.

I've never believed in this, in meeting someone and knowing right away he's the person to fight for. I've never been one of those people who has searched for butterflies in my stomach and the feeling of hearts and flowers in my life.

My cynical self is rolling her eyes at the thought that Matthias is so much more than a man I met recently, but my soul is whispering the familiarity I've longed to discover.

Matthias's face dips down to mine, his lips hovering over mine. I tilt my head up to meet him, brushing our lips together. Once. Twice. His hand no longer brushes my shoulder. Now, it tangles in my hair, keeping me close to him so his lips can explore mine unhurriedly. The tip of his tongue touches mine, and I open for him, desperate to deepen the kiss and needing to continue this lazy exploration.

I arch my body up to kiss him deeper, my tongue dancing with his, our legs a tangled mess. Matthias reaches for my hip, squeezing before pulling me to him and placing me on top of his body, our lips never missing a beat.

I moan into his mouth, feeling his body beneath me. The hand in my hair tightens its grip and I know he's holding back. Feeling his lips on mine, the sensual kisses we're sharing is making it hard for me to remain in control. His lips abandon mine and move down to my neck. My skin pebbles and my hips press down against his. A growl escapes the back of his throat and he stops his lips.

"Not yet," his voice is hoarse as he looks at me. I nod. "We'll get there."

"I know." I brush my lips against his. "I want to take our time getting there."

He hugs me to him, and I place my head on his chest, his heartbeat drumming to a beat that is uniquely his. I feel a kiss on the crown of my head. Being in his arms, held by him, feels safe. Yet, I feel the lingering monster waiting to strike and destroy this.

It's there, biding its time.

"Want to get breakfast?" Matthias breaks the silence.

"Yeah."

We sit in a small café I've never been to before. Matthias drinks tea and I drink coffee.

"How did you start writing?" he asks.

"Oh man." I look up at the ceiling. "I won't even pretend that I've been writing since I was a child and a book lover since before then. Truth is, I hated reading growing up. It wasn't until I was in college that I appreciated books. As for writing, it wasn't something I sought. I was in middle school, I think you call it secondary school here. I was thirteen and my literature teacher assigned a poetry project to finish our poetry unit. We had to analyze some poems and then write our own. I can't remember how many poems we had to write, but it was a decent amount. I was so upset about the assignment." I breathe deeply.

"Poetry isn't just something you sit and write, you know? It's born from somewhere else. I wasn't Shakespeare. I wasn't a poet, and I thought poetry was so…" I search for the right word. "Stupid." Okay, so it's not the best word.

Matthias laughs at my honesty.

"I was thirteen," I defend.

"So, what happened?" He leans on his elbows with rapt attention.

"I had to write them. I couldn't fail an assignment that would count for so much of my grade. I can't remember the first one I wrote, but one was a love poem, and I remember using the name Trevor. I have no idea why I picked it except it rhymed with the verse." I roll my eyes. "Anyway, as soon as I started writing, a flood was released. Every pain I was swallowing ripped from me onto paper without meaning to. I wrote about pain, suicide, confusion, depression. To this day, I say I owe my life to poetry. That assignment gave me something I wasn't searching for. It allowed me to express what I was hiding from the world. It gave me safety."

"Do you still write poetry?" His curiosity peaked.

"Yes. I had stopped for a while, especially when I

started writing novels. Poetry comes and goes in my life when I need it. I'm now learning to write it as something more than pain medication."

"When did you start writing novels?" His eyes are trained on mine.

"A few years ago. While I lived in Spain, I wrote a wedding scene that always stuck in my memory, but writing books wasn't in my plans. I didn't think I could ever write so many words and develop a plot. It just happened one day," I shrug.

"It's fascinating."

"Not really. I don't know. Maybe it is to someone on the outside. My friends tease that I write a ton of books in one day. It's a joke between us because I get so focused on a story, I won't stop until I finish it. I'll get lost in words for hours a day, living in fantasy land. What they don't know is that I get lost in the words to keep my sanity. I use it as an escape the way an addict uses drugs to forget their ghosts. Writing is my addiction. I hate calling it that because it's something so beautiful, something so significant to me. But I use it like I would any other substance."

"Maybe, instead of an addiction, it's your purpose. That's why you get so lost in it. You enter a different world. It helps you sort through your own struggles, even when you write what you call silly romances. If you can witness your characters overcoming their pain, you can overcome yours."

My eyes water as I hear him speak. The pressure in my chest is holding my air hostage from filling my lungs. I gasp for breath, willing my force of life to move through me and rub my eyes.

"Maybe. Right now, I want to work on my other book. I want to share what I've learned from life, in hopes that I can assist someone in their own journey. Maybe help humanity in some small way."

"You will."

I wish I could be as confident as him. I've put so much pressure on myself with this project that I'm afraid I've created a barrier between my mind and my heart. Right now, all I know for certain is that Matthias and I are stardust lovers whose paths have merged, creating both chaos and peace.

8
my truths

"I always wanted to live where the fairies were. My favorite Disney movie is *Sleeping Beauty* because of the fairies."

Matthias looks up at me from the book he's reading—yup, still mine—and wrinkles his eyes. "What about them did you love?"

"They can fly. Fairies are gorgeous and magical beings. I don't know, it was always a feeling. Was there ever anything magical that you loved growing up?"

He bookmarks the page and closes the book, letting it rest on his lap. "Maybe aliens? Although I don't know if I'd call them magical, it always intrigued me, wondering if there was life on other planets."

"And?"

"We're definitely not the only existing race in the entire universe."

"I think so, too." I turn my attention back to my laptop, feeling content with the small tidbit of myself I shared.

Matthias followed me home after breakfast, making it known he'd be spending the day with me. When I told him I was going to write, he didn't mind, he just reached for the book that was waiting for him on the coffee table and began reading. We've been here for hours, in the same space.

I stretch my legs out, my knees aching from being bent in the same position for too long, and sigh. How great would it be if beyond the depth of this world lay a magical one? This town is kind of magical in its history and mysticism.

I focus back on my document, typing out the connection I feel to my roots, no limiting beliefs, just feelings.

"Would you have preferred a German?"

"What?" I look at Matthias, his interruption confusing me.

He points to the book. "Would you have preferred a German?" he repeats.

"No." I shake my head in case my words are mute to his ears. "Why do you ask that? He's just a character."

"No character is *just* a character. You pulled him from somewhere."

"I don't prefer a German," I emphasize. Matthias and I have fallen into a comfort level in a short amount of time, as I stare at him lounging on my sofa. "However, you do remind me of him. Maybe I wrote you long before I met you. Maybe it was a way of my soul calling to you."

"I'm not like him. Not at all. I'm flawed." His nostrils flare.

"Maybe in my eyes, you aren't." I lift a brow.

"Don't look at me with those eyes, then." He stands.

"Where are you going?" I put my laptop on the table and stare at him.

"Nowhere."

"Then sit," I demand.

He begins pacing as he reads the page he has open to himself. Something has riled him up. I know better than to interject. I watch him as he continues to pace and read. Finally, he drops to the couch and places his head on my lap.

"You're not the only one experiencing emotions you've drowned beneath the sea of your memory." I brush his hair in silence. "Meeting you, all of this, it's been so quick. I haven't had time to process what seeing you in person has awoken. It's a beast I've tamed, but eventually, even the most well-trained monster betrays his master." He takes a few deep breaths, closing his eyes. I don't stop stroking his hair.

"It's as if I'm seeing and feeling the things I lived through all over again. After years of releasing it. It's a movie in my mind, except it isn't fiction."

I reach for his hand, holding him. "I understand. I've been feeling the same. Things I had thought I was done with have poked into my being, reminding me what it felt like to be afraid and confused. To not understand why it was happening. You can hate the person, but I can't, because I was a product of someone else's abuse," I voice for the first time. "I've never been able to hate because what was done to me was what was being done to him. It's how he learned what love was. It's not right or wrong. It just is. I had accepted that. Until recently."

At some point, Matthias opened his eyes while I was speaking. My own are staring at an ugly painting on the wall next to the television that I wish I could remove. I look down at him and shrug. "It is what it is. He didn't know it was wrong because he was told it was right. The person that hurt you was different. I know of those kinds of monsters, too. We all picked a role in this life, and that's a hard pill to swallow. To accept that we chose to experience certain things. Many people don't get it. They don't believe it. It's easier to judge and point fingers than grasp the idea that we needed to live through things so our soul can evolve."

I swallow loudly and finally make eye contact with him. "I hate it. I hate you lived through that. I hate that I'm the person that is stirring it awake. I'm sorry."

He turns his head toward my body and kisses my stomach. "Don't be. It's not your fault. This is part of the process. Part of being human."

I bend my body down to kiss his lips. "We've only just met, yet I feel like it's been an eternity."

"Because in a way, it has."

I smile, the tension still rolling around the room. "I want coffee," I announce.

Matthias laughs and sits up. "Let's go get some."

I don't argue. I stand, put on my shoes, and wait for him by the door. His smile lightens his face, and his body is much more relaxed. We walk down the steps and into the cool evening.

When we reach the coffee shop near my house, we take a seat and order our drinks. As always, Matthias with his tea and me with my coffee.

As soon as I decided to stop writing this perfect version of what a book that deals with spirituality should be, the words started to flow. I want people to connect to the words I want to share with them; therefore, it should be far from perfection, since none of us are perfect.

I was comparing myself to others. I was comparing what I wanted to share to how others have shared their own knowledge. I can only be myself. I can only do what I do. Being truthful will be the only way to do this. No more fiction. No more pretending I don't have the wisdom to share.

I hold my journal tighter in my hand as I cross the street. After almost an entire week without working, I was happy to see my clients today. My purse weighs down on my shoulder with the new crystals I bought. I should've left them at work, but I wanted to cleanse them after using them with people today.

I take a seat on the bench in the park. The afternoon

called for some outdoor time with the sun shining down, creating a shimmer on the damp ground. I cross my leg and place the journal on my lap, opening to the page I was working on early this morning. I get lost in the free-flowing writing.

So many times, I don't speak up. I quiet myself because I'm embarrassed to talk about topics that I assume others don't have a clue about. I want to help humanity, but I don't dare express what will help it. For a long time, I silenced my voice. I didn't want people to know what I was feeling or who I was. I hid my self-expression, replaced it with that of others, like the chameleon I am.

Now, I've decided to share it. Many won't like it. It's hard to accept a new version of someone you love. It's hard to understand the changes in people when you thought they were perfect before. This voice? This is real. This is me and I'm keeping my vow not to hide anymore. And it starts with the one thing I've always used as a shield—writing.

It's not just keeping quiet about things people did. I've silenced myself from my own being. I haven't honored who I am because I was always afraid I wouldn't be accepted. Always talking myself out of it because I'd sound crazy or get sideways glances and raised eyebrows.

I've turned into such a coward.

No. I'm brave.

It takes bravery to live, and many times I could've so easily called it quits. There were more times in my life that I wanted to die than I wanted to live, than I wanted to simply survive. I think if I weren't so afraid of blood and open flesh, I would've slit my wrists all those years ago.

My mother punished me when I would yell how badly I wanted to die. She was blind to my cry for help. I was too angry to let her know I was serious. I let her believe it was teenage rebellion. It's easier that way. *To hide.*

I used to want to kill myself, but I didn't know how I'd do it. Too much of a coward, I used to think. Not having the courage to kill yourself was cowardice. I wrote a book once and dedicated it to all those that wanted to end their lives but chose to stay. Living takes more courage than dying. Self-hatred can lead you down a path of darkness, but I finally understood the difference.

I shake my head. Lately, it's as if all the work I've done to better myself has slipped through cracks in the soil and was burned by the heat of the Earth's molten core. I feel as if I'm taking steps back, being pulled by the things that hurt me for so long. Things I used to hurt myself.

I know better.

A dull sound comes from my bag on the bench, thankfully steering my mind away from sullen thoughts. I search for my phone, digging through the crystals and past my wallet.

"Hello?" My exhale is heavy as a smile creeps on my face.

"Hi. Are you done with work?" Matthias's deep voice echoes in my ear.

"Yes. I finished some time ago."

"Oh. So you're free?" he questions.

"Yes…" I wait for him to say what he wants directly.

"I'll pick you up. I want to cook you dinner."

"At your place?" I've yet to see where he lives.

"Yes."

"Give me a bit to get home. I'm at the park near Chalice Well," I explain as nerves move through me.

"I'll pick you up in an hour," he states, confident and eager.

We hang up and I stand, heading home to get ready to see Matthias. To see where he lives.

Matthias lives in the countryside. A small cottage with land surrounding it. This is a part of town I've not seen yet since I haven't wandered out this far. The steep-sloped roof adds a unique character to the design. The home feels like it's out of a storybook. The white walls are textured inside and out.

It's an adorable home.

"This was my grandparents' home. I inherited it a few years ago," he explains as we enter.

"It's beautiful." I look around, catching the brick fireplace in the living room, flanked by floor to ceiling bookcases on both sides. Cozy doesn't even begin to describe this space. Matthias walks up behind me, wrapping his arms around my body. He kisses the crown of my head.

"I love it here, and it's still close to the town center. No more than a short drive, but I have privacy. I have peace."

I nod. He does have all that. On the drive over, I noticed a few sheep grazing in a field. It reminded me of Spain.

"What do you want to drink?" he asks as he releases me.

"Just water, please." He nods and walks into the kitchen. I follow him. The wooden cabinets are painted ivory and the countertop contrasts slightly with a natural wood top. It's small, yet open with a tall, rustic table sitting in the middle, acting as an island.

"How can I help?"

"Want to help me peel potatoes? I'm making roast beef and roast potatoes."

"Sounds good. Just point me to the potatoes and

peeler," I smile, a sense of want for something I've never truly desired overcoming me.

Matthias gets me set up in a section of the counter and gets to work preparing the meat. I tell him about my day, my writing.

"Do you mind if I have a drink?" he asks.

"Not at all. Why would I?"

"I've noticed you don't drink." He shrugs as he reaches for the amber liquid in the top cabinet.

"I have nothing against alcohol, I just don't drink it as much anymore."

"How come?"

I have an addictive personality. Always have. It's easier to sink into an outside substance than to have a clear vision of the ugliness I carry. My favorite vice was always alcohol. I knew the moment an amber liquid hit my lips, just like the one Matthias is serving himself, I wouldn't stop until I forgot. Until I shut up my subconscious. The mind is easy to manipulate with a new dress or jewelry. With the falseness of social media—one status update with lying words that prove to the world how amazing your life is. The mind is the easiest to convince, but the subconscious . . . The subconscious holds the truth. A light buzz wouldn't shut it down, so I'd drink until everything faded except for the pungent taste of alcohol sitting on my tongue.

"I used to get drunk to numb the pain. I drank to forget," I confess.

"So, you quit?" His eyebrows furrow.

I shrug. "I simply don't need it anymore. I don't need to run from the truth by drowning it in a black hole of alcohol. If I desire a drink, I have one. I no longer want to *use* it as I had done for so long. That doesn't serve me." The feeling of waking up with a groggy state of unknowingness always weighed heavy on me.

"I agree. It should be for pleasure, but not a necessity."

I nod, biting the inside of my cheek.

I embarrassed myself the last time I got drunk. Actually, I don't know if I did. I can't remember. It's all a blur, pieces of the day flashing behind my eyes like the pictures I'd snapped crossing the screen of my phone. I was out for a birthday. Day drinking. That was my favorite. I hadn't drank in months, finally owning who I was, pulling myself out of the mess that is my life, sober. But I love day drinking. Beer, champagne, whiskey. Any excuse to savor the bitter alcohol on my lips.

It took one comment. One hurtful comment for me to succumb to the numbness. The sting was greater than the guilt of drinking. The guilt of going against my will.

People can be hateful. They love to look at the negative in other people's lives instead of acknowledging their wins. We all struggle. We all hurt. Why must we be the purpose of that pain instead of the foundation to build each other up?

I wore the coat of embarrassment and shame for days afterward, avoiding those I was with. Avoiding myself. Instead, I lay in a bed of self-loathing, hating myself more with each minute that passed. I couldn't emerge from the punishment I was imposing on myself. It was a cold, bitter cycle. If no one was going to punish me, I'd do it myself. It buried me.

The hurtful words of someone else led me down a path of self-destruction. I vowed never again. I vowed never to let someone else make me feel inferior. But that vow is difficult to keep when I was already feeling less than. The words tipped me over so quickly because I had brought myself down to that place. The alcohol I consumed was the excuse to blame someone else.

As much as I enjoy a drink, I had to come to realize I wasn't consuming it healthily. I was spiraling out of control. It went from two glasses of wine to an entire bottle on a Wednesday night, because #WineWednesday. It went from two scotches to five and getting in a car to drive home. I was purposefully placing myself in dangerous situations. Testing my fate. Playing between the risk of invincibility and mortality.

When I started to feel sick from just a sip of beer, I knew I had to take a step back, especially if I wanted to heal my wounds. The alcohol would just feed the flesh that was begging to be cared for. My heart was begging for me to listen, for me to face my issues so I can overcome them. But my mind was begging for the alcohol to quiet the heart.

When it all snapped into place, I no longer craved the need to drink away my anger. I can't say what exactly happened. I just woke up one day with a knowingness that I no longer wanted to drink to forget. I wanted to remember, so I could embrace my truths and own them.

"If I ever want to enjoy a drink, I will," I tell Matthias.

"I respect that." He smiles and winks. I relax and finish preparing the potatoes.

After dinner, we sit on a thick blanket on the living room floor with the flames of the fireplace dancing before us. I love his home. I would never want to leave this place if I lived here.

I yawn and stretch my arms in front of me. Matthias pulls me closer to his chest.

"Do you want to stay?" he asks before kissing my temple.

"I work tomorrow morning."

"I'll take you home and then drop you off at work."

"Are you sure?" The depth of his blue eyes draws me in.

"Of course." His eyes are bright with the reflection of the flames dancing in them.

I lean in and kiss him. "Okay," I say against his lips.

He guides us to his bedroom, handing me a tee shirt to change into.

Once I'm ready, I lie next to him and enjoy the warmth of his heat surrounding my body.

9

the saint in red

My body tenses and I awaken. I inhale the scent of pine and Matthias. His skin is wrapped around me as my nose breathes in his bare chest. I twist away from him and search for my phone on the bedside table. Seeing the time, I sneak out of bed and tiptoe around the dark house, using my phone as a guiding light.

I unlock the door with the key hanging from the lock and step out into the cold night. Out here, the sky shines brighter with the shimmering stars that move around in the universe, worlds away. They show off their beauty. If I didn't love them so much, I'd be offended by their boastful exhibition.

I walk out from the stoop and onto the grass, wet from the evening dew. I should've gone back to sleep, seeing as it's three in the morning, but I'm a lover of the night. Doing this helps center me. After spending the night in Matthias' house, sleeping in the same bed, which is more intimate than sex can be, with my soul painted on my skin for him to read as he pleases, I need to ground myself. So much, so fast.

That's how it is when you meet your twin flame. But I'd be a fool to think it will always be this easy and the anxiety that vibrates inside of me, knowing it won't be, keeps me awake at night.

I breathe in, sucking down the cool air, and staring up at the sky. With the clusters of stars much more evident here, I wish I were living in a place where the stars were within reach. A planet far away, where pain no longer exists because the beings that inhabit it have already overcome the density of humanity.

I shiver and stick my arms in through the shirt sleeves, wishing I had grabbed a jacket.

"I thought you might be here." His voice is gruff with sleep.

I keep my arms crossed around me, hugging my body inside the shirt. "Ever since I was a little girl, I've loved the stars. Back home, I couldn't appreciate them, but I'd still search for them. When I'd visit Spain, I'd spend hours outside under the night sky, neck craned back, counting and staring at those mysterious specks. There's something in me that's called to them." I don't turn around to look at him. I know he's approaching.

"Like fairies?" his voice is teasing.

"More." I turn to look at him, eyes wide.

The soft smile that adorns his face paints my heart in vibrant colors.

Finally.

"Tell me everything about you."

"You already know a lot."

"But I want to know it all. Tell me about The Saint in Red."

I stop. Freeze. The cold air is warm in comparison to his request. My heart halts. "How do you know he's real?"

"Because you write about him with such emotion, it's impossible he's not." His keen intuition is too aligned with my life.

"Was."

"What?"

"Was. He's dead now," I state indifferently.

"The emotion is still very much alive, though," he

points out.

I nod. "When I wrote that book, I didn't know the extent of it. He was just someone that did a horrific thing. Now, I know it goes beyond that. The more time that passes, the more I learn that it wasn't one horrific mistake. It was…" I shake my head, tears welling in my eyes. "He ruined so much for me. I used to love my family. Now," I shrug. "It was all a lie."

I hate him because he ruined the idea I had of my family. I thought we were a family worth being proud of. I realize now it's bullshit. How could you stand by that? How could you live that way? Damaging people, children.

I hate him.

I hate him.

I hate him.

He died of a stroke. Home alone. On his way to the bathroom. Everyone cried and mourned the amazing man.

I couldn't cry. My delayed reaction to situations didn't allow me to. I remember one of my cousins telling me it was okay to cry, thinking it was my pride holding back the waterfall. In retrospect, I think a part of my subconscious knew the kind of man he was.

He may have been a good grandpa, but he was a shitty father. And now, I think every memory I have of him is tainted by sickness.

"Do you really want to know?" I ask Matthias.

"Yes."

"It won't be easy. I'm not done processing it all," I warn.

"I won't push more than you can go." He reaches his hand out to me and I stare at it. Sneaking one arm out from the shirt, I hold onto his hand and walk closer to him.

"Don't let go," I whisper.

We settle in front of the fireplace after Matthias sparks the flames back to life and makes us tea.

Wrapped up in a blanket, I sip the tea before speaking.

"When I was a little girl, I used to be so happy. I was this rebellious child, fearless. I used to believe my family was perfect. Not perfect-perfect, but perfect for me. Perfect in my eyes. I knew we had flaws, but they weren't anything that would ruin us. It was so far from the truth. I had no idea what the foundation of our family was really built on." I drink more tea, swallowing with it the hatred I'm feeling.

"Anyway, things happened not long after that did change me. But back to my grandfather, my mom's dad. I call him The Saint in Red because he was oh, so holy. A Catholic man with enviable morals and a good heart." My dry laughter emphasizes my sarcasm. Matthias is patient as I get this all out. "I hate him so much," my breathing catches. "He was a sick fuck. He abused children. His children. Not a touch here or a touch there. He forced one to…" I lean my head back and close my eyes. "Some things are hard to voice." I swallow hard.

"He had to have been sick. There's no other way around it. Yet, I don't think he was the only one in his generation to be this way. I think they were all fucked up. I was once told the men used to go hunting and would take their sons with them. Hunting wasn't the only thing they would do. It makes me sick to know he makes up part of my DNA. It makes me angry."

Tears roll down my face like silent pleas to escape this ancestral imprisonment.

"I come from that man because without him, I wouldn't be here," my voice rises. "I don't want to be associated to him. He was supposed to be our family foundation. He was supposed to be the pillar that holds us up. His support crumbled when I learned he was nothing but a son of a bitch. He failed me. He failed us all. He allowed this snowball effect to happen in our family. He allowed the patterns to repeat themselves. He ruined my childhood by being a sick fuck."

My body trembles uncontrollably as silent tears turn into begging sobs. I drop the mug on the floor, some of the tea splashing around me, and dig my hands in my head, tugging the roots of my hair.

Instantly, Matthias wraps me in his arms, holding me.

I don't want his touch to feel good.

I don't want his touch to remind me of unwanted touches.

I don't want any of this confusion and mixed emotions.

Good.

Bad.

Wrong.

Right.

He's not the person who hurt me, so I allow him to comfort me, but any touch right now reminds me of too much. He senses my discomfort but doesn't let go. It's not aimed at him. It's aimed at my past. It's aimed at the broken girl. The life my grandfather led catapulted into energetic cycles of abuse in our family

"I hate him so much," I whisper. My body limp and my chest aching with unfinished pressure.

"The hatred will kill you," Matthias speaks into my hair. "But I know that kind of pain."

"How could my grandmother stay, knowing the monster she was sleeping next to?"

For a long time, I was angry at my grandmother for choosing to continue to sleep next to the monster she had uncovered. How could she? How could she stay knowing what he had done, possibly what he continued to do? How could she choose him over her children?

When I think of my family now, I think of failure. I think of disgust.

When I think of my grandfather, only one thing comes to mind: sick fuck.

Because who I thought was a great man, was nothing more than a twisted bastard living in a shadow. Every memory is now marked with the knowledge that he . . .

I swallow back bile. I once asked my aunt if she thought he had hurt any of his grandchildren. She said she didn't. That was left for his children. But we were screwed regardless because of the stamp he engraved in our DNA.

"I don't know. We can't understand people's decisions or motives, and they're not for us to judge."

"Everything I thought I knew. Everything I believed he was, is shattered. The man I admired so much. He had to have been sick, right?" I look up at Matthias.

He shrugs. "I don't know. We don't understand why people do things. We don't have to understand why people come into our lives with certain roles. We simply need to understand that they do."

"I come from a line of red sinners and conforming preachers. It's easier to speak of good and evil, judging others, to silence the disgust you're living. To hide. No one ever knows what really happens behind shut blinds and dark rooms in the middle of the night."

"You are not him."

"I'm not." I shake my head with conviction. "But his actions led to a thread of hurt and heartache for a lot of us." I stare at the fire and suck in its heat. "When others talk about the great man he was, I walk out of the room. I look at the reaction of the few people who know the truth, waiting for one of us to explode."

"But it's not your right."

I shake my head. "It's not. It's not my truth to unveil, no matter how much it did affect me. I wasn't a direct victim of his. Over the years, the anger has been bubbling low in the base of my spine. I didn't even feel it. I didn't know I had it. One day it snapped free, knocking me down and throwing chaos at me like confetti at a five-year-old's party. It broke me. The anger."

"What caused it?"

"I don't know. It just happened. I saw things as more than they were. As the truth. The masks must've taunted me, and I tore them off, seeing the distorted faces behind them. The realization that all I lived was a lie hit me until I was on the ground, lifeless. It was all too much at once." I can't catch my breath.

"Maybe you were ready to battle it?" Matthias suggests.

"Maybe." I know we heal in phases. It could be that it was time I heal this. It was time I looked at my family roots for what they were. The ultimate test of forgiveness will either end the cycle for good, so I can release from this bullshit, or break me into dust that will never be recovered.

"Why use the term The Saint in Red?"

"Because he lived in false holiness, stained by sins."

Church on Sundays, prayers before bed, talk about God and attending retreats. He lived the face of religious honor. It's why I turned away from religious institutions and stayed with my personal beliefs. No manipulations or nasty actions to feel an egotistical power. Demons eventually get exposed in the bright sun of a new day.

"Sleep, love." Matthias's voice soothes me as my eyes close. I cling on tight when he carries me to the room. I stay wrapped in him until the sun rises, and I awaken to the softness of his fingers caressing my skin.

"Good morning."

"Hi." I clear my throat and look over his shoulder, to the sketch hanging on his wall. "Did you draw that?"

"Yes." He doesn't look, knowing what I'm talking about.

"It's beautiful." The simple pencil lines create beautiful scenery of tall forest trees.

"Thank you."

"How long have you been drawing?" I scoot away enough to look at him.

"Since I was a boy. It came naturally to me," he shrugs.

"Don't pretend like it's no big deal. You're talented."

He nods once. "How are you feeling?"

"Like I was hit by a train. It's going to be a long day." Last night was the first time I spoke about my grandfather. Before then, it was all internal. Swallowing more and more, unable to speak about it.

"Reschedule your appointments."

"I have people counting on me," I respond.

"You can't just ignore your own process." Matthias's words are demanding.

"I'm not, but life goes on. I have to work." I'm firm in my decision.

"Get dressed then, or you'll be late." He sits up and moves to stand, his voice ringing with annoyance. I grab his hand and pull him back, catching him off guard. He falls back onto the bed. I lean up on an elbow and stare at his eyes.

"Thank you." I brush my lips with his. "Thank you for letting me speak. Thank you for listening." His hand finds my hip under my tee shirt and squeezes.

"You're welcome."

I place my hand on his chest, holding my body up, slightly over his. His heart thumps under my hand, its vibrations moving up my arm and through me, beating a different kind of life into me.

My eyes remain on his, both unblinking. His other hand brushes the wavy mess from my face. Neither of us needs to speak to know how deeply we feel for each other. This isn't like past relationships. This one has no rules and all the rules under the universe at the same time. This relationship will break us and rebuild us. I just hope we're both strong enough to stay when it's all done.

10
ho'oponopono

I stare at the doodles in my journal. This isn't exactly what I thought I'd do when I grabbed my journal to write. Instead of words, I drew multiple designs of the next tattoo I want to get done—a crescent moon with sun rays inside. The pen is set between my fingers like a cigarette, what once was a familiar hold for me. I exhale. That was one thing I quit cold turkey after a health scare.

I lean my head against the glass door that leads to the inside of my apartment. The day is dreary, but I wanted to sit out on the balcony. This kind of weather brings serenity into my life. Even gray brings color into some people's lives. I'm one of those people. It's unfortunate some think rainy days are curses from the sky. I long for days like this. It restores my soul.

After last night's storytelling and emotional sprints, I needed this.

I smile as the cold raindrops tickle my feet that are propped on the railing. I stare at the garden below as the flowers and leaves dance with the rain. Finding this place to live in at an affordable price was a stroke of serendipity. When things are meant to work out, they will, no matter how impossible it seems. Making the choice to move here began a snowball effect until the path to arrive was so perfectly aligned, I had questioned its reality.

It was a brave move, to leave and go somewhere I'd never been. I'd only ever seen pictures online, but my soul was being called. I felt nostalgic for something I never had—a longing for a love that I wasn't familiar with yet completely consumed in. *More than a soulmate.*

I reach for my mug and notice it's empty. Right now, I'd kill for powers where I can refill my coffee while sitting here on the balcony. Since I'm not a qualified telekinesis pro, I stand and shake the water from my feet.

I ignore the mess of papers in the living room as I pass on my way to the kitchen and warm up milk. The peace I feel now is the aftereffect of the enraged monster that shattered my rational mind an hour ago. I tore papers I had saved since I was thirteen. All my poems destroyed, shredded with the sharp nails of a lonely wolf who lives for the nights she can howl at the moon. After, I packed up my grief and shipped it away in a carriage, along with the poem I found that caused the spiral.

When I was fifteen, my Spanish teacher told us about a contest at the county fair. It was open to everyone in the class. Write a poem in Spanish to submit. By the time she finished explaining what we had to do, I had the poem written in my binder.

It was about the incredible man who was so loved. The man who was perfect. The person who was the example to live by.

I gag as the microwave beeps.

I remove the mug, add coffee to the hot milk, and swallow a chug, burning the bile back into the acid of my stomach.

That copy of the poem no longer exists. Its words will never mock me again. Not after today.

Years later, I made a scrapbook page with his picture and the poem. That one survived tonight's storm. I have no idea where I packed it, but it's only a matter of time before every false memory I have of my grandfather is destroyed. Only truths from now on.

I make my way back to the balcony and regain the same position, feet propped, body relaxed. Not a care in the world but the strength of this coffee.

Destruction can be a therapeutic technique.

I grab the journal again and begin writing.

For so long I've lived in fear. An emotion engraved in me, along with lacking. Fear of failure. Fear of having everything I've desired. Fear of never having enough. Fear of losing love. Fear of being too loved, that it would suffocate me. Every fear I had pushed away every desire I wanted. Now I get it. When your backbone is weak, when you lose that support, you lose it all.

Losing my paternal grandfather at a young age left me vulnerable. Later in life, learning my maternal grandfather was a sick fuck left me broken. Both male pillars abandoned me in some way.

Without those pillars, it's difficult to live abundantly. It's difficult to be open to a man, trusting he wouldn't leave me as well. That I wouldn't end up with the same monster others had. The girl inside of me has been sad for so long.

I never grieved my paternal grandfather's death. I never faced it. It was easier to put on a mask and play dress-up. Except, this was real life, not a play. There are no dress rehearsals this time. Not unless I want to continue in the same cycle until the day my ashes are spread across the river in my father's village.

Our roots, our ancestors, are our foundation for strength, yet we come into this life to heal the lineage. I remember my abuse so I can heal it, yet I've hidden it, covered it, too afraid of what it would do.

But was it abuse? For so long I thought so until I learned the reason why. We all came with this stamp on our body, victim or perpetrator. Some were both. We continued to fall into it. No one was taking the step to say, enough. *Now we're saying it. Those of us who remember. We can break the chains, but it starts with us.*

107

How many generations does it take to end the pain?

I smile, placing the pen in the center of the journal. I know what I need to write.

The messy cursive scribbled on the pale blue pages hold the answer I've been seeking when it comes to this book. All I had to do was let go and write as Matthias said.

Through all of this, I know I need to forgive. Maybe I need to forgive myself for choosing this life because my human mind doesn't understand my soul's contract.

Ho'oponopono.

I write a lot of bullshit. A hypocrite. I make my characters heal what I don't bother looking into. It's not enough to make the fictional people do the healing for me. They're only a part of me. As much as I think writing those characters helps dissolve my pain, it's only a fraction of what I need to do. I can't hide behind words like I've been doing for almost twenty years.

I need to own it.

My chest expands with air and my lungs fill before slowly deflating like a week-old balloon. I inhale again and blow the breath through my mouth.

Eyes shut and black takes over, soft shots of light dancing behind my lids. One more breath, a meaningful one this time, takes over.

In my head, I say: *I'm sorry. Please forgive me. I love you. Thank you.*

I repeat the phrases that vibrate with ho'oponopono's depth. This is for me. Not for the monster, who I've grown to hate. Not for my grandmother, who stood silent. Not for my mother, or my father, or my aunts, or my cousins, or my brother. This is for me.

I visualize the little girl I was, repeating the mantras until I'm crying against my hands, wanting to scream but staying mute. That's how I felt as a child. Raging inside, but quiet on the outside. Taught that the image we give off must be perfect, so those wanting to scrutinize us don't see our flaws.

In Spanish, we call that *el qué dirán*. Everything is for appearance's sake. Fix yourself before others judge you. Before others see the cracks. Perfect your makeup and hair. Always put together, clothes ironed, shoes clean—wiping away the stains we stepped in on the way out. *Because what was inside, was far from what was shown on the outside.*

I open my eyes. So much for working on forgiveness. I sigh. It won't happen in five minutes. It won't happen in five days. It will happen one day when I allow myself to forgive. Sometimes it's easier to hold on to the pain.

Whatever caused this fountain to burst made sure it all came out at once. *I was doing so well.* I laugh at my thought. We're constantly learning in this life. I wasn't done because I merely had some months of intense peace and happiness. That was the calm before the storm. Right now, I'm in the eye of the hurricane, and soon those walls surrounding the eye will knock on my soul.

Checking the time on my phone, I decide to go to bed. Sleep will help calm my mind. Rest will help me center. I leave the scraps of paper on the living room floor. I'll throw them away tomorrow when I'm not pretending I don't care. When I'm not pretending at all. Today, I needed to allow myself a moment of falsehood so I can gather myself.

Okay, pretending isn't the best word. I numbed and I silenced myself so I could find a few minutes of peace. When I did, I wrote, and there I discovered what I need to share.

⟋⟍

I inhale the musty vapor that fills the air as I walk

around town. I've been wandering since I left work an hour ago, thinking about what I told the last client I had, who is working on forgiving her first husband. The universe likes to throw us situations that mirror our own. I may not have a first husband to forgive, but I do have a lot of unsettled ghosts to make peace with. I have an entire generation to bow to, thank, forgive, and release.

Makenna noticed something in me, but she remained quiet. I'm glad. I wouldn't have had the energy to discuss anything with her right now. I need to be with myself at the moment, reflect and work through this. One thing I'm certain of is that I'm done gripping onto the pain. I want to feel so I can release. I want to move forward from this lighter.

I'm supposed to meet Matthias and a few of his friends tonight. I almost canceled because it's easier, and besides, I love running. There's comfort when it's just Matthias and me, but when we bring in the outside world, I question how we will be as individuals and as one. But alas, I can't be a hermit. That's not why I moved. I've been a hermit for far too long, and now it's time I live.

I smile at a few faces as I pass them on the street, following the same circular path I've been on since I left work. When my phone alerts me of a new message from Matthias asking if I'm nearby, I take a few calming breaths and make my way to the pub.

I see Matthias as soon as I crack the door open. His presence will always be the first I sense in any room. It's a draw. It's a tie between us. His eyes find mine immediately and his full lips curve up at the ends. He doesn't wait for me to reach him. He comes my way and meets me in the middle.

"Are you okay?" His intuition reads me. I nod. "Come on." He holds my hand and walks me to the table where his friends are. He introduces me to all of them. There's a Nick and a James. An Emily and a Tom and an Anne. I'll keep them straight in my mind after I interact with them a bit. Right now, I forgot which name belongs to which face.

I'm asked questions about the States, my choice to move here when I had sunny skies and clear beaches within reach. I listen to them talk and tease each other, getting swept away in their accent and not understanding half of the slang they use. But I laugh at their camaraderie. It's clear they've known each other for a long time, since kids. They have a strong bond.

Matthias keeps his hand on my leg, holding me intimately as his hand wraps around my thigh and squeezes the inside of my knee randomly throughout the night. When he catches me staring at his drink, he leans in and asks if I want one. While I contemplate saying yes, I shake my head. I feel better when I'm sober.

His smile is light, and I shiver when his lips graze my cheek.

Emily sighs and smiles. "You two are just lovely together." She clasps her hands and rests her chin on them. "Aren't they, Anne?"

I try to hide my blush, but the heat increases before I can control it.

"You're embarrassing her," James says.

Oh God. My smile is tight to keep my emotions in check.

"Bugger off," she tells James. "All I'm saying is that I'm so happy Matthias met you," Emily looks at me. "He was driving us mad with all the talk about never meeting someone." Her smile is mischievous.

"I was not," Matthias defends.

"You were a total wanker, mate," Nick adds to Emily's

teasing.

I laugh at them, catching Matthias's smile.

After we eat and talk, we all go our separate way. Fingers tangled, Matthias leads me to his car. Once outside my building, he looks at me and says, "Can I stay?"

"Of course."

I laugh when he grabs a bag from the back seat. He simply shrugs. "I packed it just in case."

"Let's go," I shake my head, but my smile is etched on my face.

As soon as we enter, I'm reminded of the shreds of paper I didn't have time to clean this morning. I squeeze my eyes shut and turn to face him, my nose scrunched.

"What happened?"

I suck my lips into my mouth and bite down. "Don't worry about the living room when you see it," I warn.

Matthias's eyebrows shoot up, and he moves around me and goes into the living room. His hands are in his pocket as he assesses the mess. I remain still by the doorframe that leads to the living room, waiting for his reaction. When he turns around, sad eyes find mine. He tilts his head and nods, silently communicating.

"Let's go to bed." He doesn't say anything about the disaster. He doesn't ask questions. He doesn't judge. He simply grabs his bag from the floor at the entrance and walks into my bedroom, already changing by the time I catch up.

I'm silent as I change, mirroring his confidence in hopes it will seep into me. Inside, I'm trembling with self-judgment.

Once Matthias is ready, he walks up to me, places his hands on my hips, and leans down to kiss me.

"Thank you for coming tonight. I know my friends made fun of me, but they weren't wrong. For a long time, I was searching for you. Not someone like you, but *you*. I knew the more I searched, the less I'd find you. I had to let go of my need to seek someone and enjoy life. As soon as I did, you were here, in front of me. I know you're dealing with things, but it's so we can become free of those emotional scars and live our life together."

"I know," I whisper. "It's worth it." I get on my toes and kiss his lips, holding him to me.

I don't want to sleep tonight. Tonight, I want to love.

Matthias's hands move from my hips to my back, pulling my body up until my legs wrap around him and he sits on the bed. I take my time to explore the ridges of his lips. I take my time to taste his tongue when it peeks out for me. His hands hold me in place, close to his body. Then they travel up the sides at a turtle's speed, feeling every inch.

I deepen the kiss when I feel his fingers graze the sides of my breasts. I'm humming from something inexplicable. This isn't like other times with past lovers. Matthias isn't just a lover.

Next thing I know, he's swept my shirt over my head and tipped me onto my back, pinning me with his body.

"You know what you mean to me. We don't need words, but in case you're uncertain, we have a love that's more than this physical world. More than other lives. It traces back to our creation. You're a part of me." His lips crash onto mine, and I wrap my body around his, merging until we're one.

11
twin flames

Throughout my journey, I've learned about twin flames. I've been in conversations where the difference between a twin flame and a soulmate is discussed. I've read about them. I've meditated and dreamt with mine. We've connected on a soul level. What I couldn't fathom was what it would be like to physically feel my twin flame.

Last night, I felt him so deep, he penetrated my soul.

Making love to Matthias was what intimacy was born to be. No words to explain the power, the connection.

Every past decision, every lesson, was put into perspective. They all led me here. I refuse to wish I had no one else in my past so that Matthias can be the only man I love in this lifetime. No. I'm grateful I had others before him. I'm grateful I've felt other hands on my body. Without them, I wouldn't have experienced what was necessary to be here.

Nights of pain, questioning why a man didn't want me, were worth it if I learned a lesson in the end. I've not always made the best decisions. I've allowed fear and ego to rule me. I've turned to desperation. If all of that helped me grow, it was worth it. It's all been worth it.

With Matthias, I can't hold back. Our connection is too deep. He would know, he would feel it.

His hair tickles my thighs as he shifts. Matthias picked me up from work and brought me home. We've been quiet. His head is on my lap as he reads while I write, using the arm of the sofa as my table.

Writing in my journal has proven to be more productive than my laptop. Journaling has always allowed me to express the inner darkness I carry. It makes sense this book wants to be written in the same way.

"Are you hungry?" Matthias looks at me when my stomach growls.

"I guess I am. I hadn't stopped to think about it."

"I'll make something." He lifts his head to stand.

"You don't have to." I stop him.

He swings his legs and sits up, leaning in to kiss me. "Keep writing. I'll call you when our food is ready."

I've never felt such peace or comfort with another human being before. Not friends, not family. I'm very reserved. My friends know this about me. All I get from them is, *If you need to talk, I'm here.* They know not to push, and I don't offer anything up easily. It's different with Matthias. He doesn't push, but I want to open. I want to bleed the filth. I want him to do the same. If we cut our bodies from the top of our heads down our center until our skin fell open like an unnecessary winter coat on a summer day, our core would be the same. Our essence is the same. We vibrate to the same beat.

I wish I could explain it in words, but this is something that surpasses logical thought and lives in an ethereal world.

We're so much more than bones and skin.

I remind myself of that when the anger consumes me. I'm more than this flesh.

I may come from the roots I'm writing about, but my soul surpasses that to another dimension, another reality not weighed down by dense energy and broken people seeking to understand their pain.

∾

I lie awake as Matthias's soft snoring fills my ears. He's

been asleep for a few hours. I've not been able to rest. My mind is racing for a finish line that I can't see. My heart is beating in rhythm to the one next to me, despite the inner-turmoil attempting to destroy my peace.

Self-sabotage. I'm too familiar with it. Right now, I feel it clenching my stomach. It whispers that this will end. That one day I'll wake up to an empty bed and the fading ghost of a man I once knew.

Not with Matthias. Not this time. We have a different purpose in the world than to cause pain with separation. Now that I've found him, I'm determined to beat the insecurities.

Not everyone leaves.

Some people stay. Some people fight. Some people are meant to live a forever by your side. He's that person. Within the struggles that we are facing and will face, we have a purpose.

I link my fingers with his that are wrapped around my stomach and hold on. I close my eyes and chase rest.

"Do you remember other lives?" I look at Matthias sitting across from me on the blanket in the meadow in front of his house. I had the afternoon free, and he's all caught up with his clients, so he brought us here, made us lunch, and set up a blanket outside.

"Some. Mostly through meditation."

"I do, too. I have a few where I lost my husband or partner, I'm not sure if we were married. It marked me. I believe it's why I've been so guarded. It goes beyond just what I've experienced here. My fear of abandonment is etched in my soul."

"We repeat experiences until we learn them. It's time you learn that no one truly abandons you. More importantly, that you don't abandon yourself. Remember, we all project onto others. If you project those fears, people will act on them. You'll attract that experience again by feeding the energy."

I nod. I know all of this in theory, but when it's our own life, it's harder to keep in check.

"Besides, now that you're aware of that, you can release it," Matthias adds.

"What do you remember of your past?" I lay on my stomach and rest my chin on my hands.

"Bits and pieces. Once I was a poor boy living in slums. Another time I wasn't the best kind of person. I carried a lot of darkness. While working on this life's struggles, I realized the man who abused me was in a past life with me." He has a faraway look as he remembers what brought him to this moment.

"How did you overcome it? The abuse." I ask hesitantly.

His eyes regain focus on mine. "I'm still overcoming it." He gives a sad smile, and I can picture him as a child, hurting. I crawl toward him and sit on his lap, holding him.

"It sucks."

He chuckles at my expression. "It does, but it makes us stronger if we choose to swim above it."

"It does. Sometimes the rip current threatens us, but if we surrender, we eventually emerge."

"Surrender," he throws the word out, testing its sound in the open air. "That's the key to life, isn't it?"

"Yeah, but as humans, we're so conditioned to control."

"The dangerous power—control."

I nod, keeping my arms around his body. He squeezes me when my breath tickles his neck. I drop a soft kiss there.

Then another right below his ear. His arms twitch again, tightening around my waist.

"We just need to trust that we're guided on the path that will help our spiritual growth," I whisper in his ear. My body tingles, being like this with him. No barriers. No fears. No confusion. Unconditional love.

"Navia…" His voice is gruff. His hands skim my back, my skin vibrating from his touch. I don't answer. I move my face to catch his lips, to share our breath. I'm ultra aware of everything—where his hands are, the feel of his tongue against mine, how his skin feels when I claw my nails into his back. When he moves us, so his body can cover mine.

All that matters in this moment is Matthias and me. Our connection. Our intimacy.

I call out when he enters me, digging my nails deeper into his back. I've never felt something like this. It's more than physical pleasure. It's our body connecting, aligning our souls, our energy.

We stare at each other's eyes as we both climax together. *In unison.*

As we catch our breaths, Matthias lowers my scrunched up shirt. I release his back, allowing his own shirt to return to its proper place.

His lips are soft when they kiss me this time. His eyes look into mine and he smiles.

"I'd always thought people exaggerated when they spoke of the connection between twin flames. Now I know it sounded cheesy because no concrete understanding of it exists, so any explanation sounds like they're trying to sell a fairytale."

"Fairytales don't compare to this," he says. "Don't run," he murmurs against my neck.

"I'm trying not to."

He leans up on his arms, his body still over mine. "I can't control what you do, but know I'm not leaving you."

I nod. Sometimes our life circumstances separate us. I don't tell him this. I don't voice my concerns. If I keep them to myself, they won't manifest. *I lie to myself.*

I cup his face. "I love you, Matthias. You know that. I've done a lot of work to be who I truly am for when I met you. That doesn't mean there isn't baggage that needs purging."

"We both have it."

With a final kiss, he moves from my body, and we both put on our jeans.

12
mirror, mirror

"How is it going?" Makenna asks as I sit on the sofa in the office after dropping a feather in the small bowl I forgot about this morning.

"Good." I scrunch up the sleeves on my sweater. It's warm in here. "Why?"

"Just checking in. You seem a little distracted."

I nod. "I'm processing things." Makenna doesn't know much about my life, but I'm sure she could intuitively weed out pieces of me.

"If you want to talk, you know I'm available. Even if it's to offer some tools to help with the process."

"Thank you. I'll take you up on that soon."

"Good. Now, how's Matthias?" She smiles mischievously.

"Things are good. We're in that phase where everything seems perfect. It's not though, and we're both aware of that. We're both working through things that have surfaced."

"When we meet someone with such deep soul connections, shifts always occur. Don't resist. Feel the emotions coming to you and have compassion with yourself. You're on the right track. Remember that when it feels like you can't handle it all," she shares.

"Thank you, Makenna."

"My pleasure, darling." She smiles and stands. "I'm going to do some work."

I nod and stand. "I'm done for today, so I'm heading

out."

I walk out into the drizzling afternoon and cover my head with my hoody. People are walking by, in and out of cafés and pubs. Some walking with shopping bags in hand. I love seeing this town with people despite the weather. I head to the crystal shop to buy incense.

I look at the different gems, each in their unique color and cut. I can't help but admire what the earth gives us when I walk into a crystal shop. I take a selenite and the incense I came for and pay before my purse weighs a ton with the amount of stone I'd want to buy.

I check my phone, noticing I've neglected my social media lately. I sweep through my notifications, responding to messages. I see one from my aunt and open it. A video about Family Constellations, the new method I recently introduced at work. I save it to watch when I'm home.

One of the hardest things I've ever done was tell her what happened to me. I never meant to. It was one of those things I swore I'd take to my grave. Secrets only weigh us down. They go peeling pieces of us until we've lost our core. They destroy us. Keeping secrets holds us back from living authentically transparent. I've clung on to it for fear of what someone would think if they knew. Possessive of my secret.

Letting it slip from my tongue almost broke me. I was working too hard to protect others I didn't' realize it would free me instead. It would free them. As soon as I spoke it aloud, so many doors opened in my life. I see now that one of the reasons I was able to make this leap is due to that expression.

As I continue to scroll through my social media, I notice a few messages from friends I haven't taken the time to answer. I wish I had an excuse, but I don't.

I'm not a good friend. I want to be, but I get too caught up in my own stuff to be. I become greedy for my own space that I forget about them. I forget to call or text. I'll think about it at three in the morning and forget come sunrise. I make plans and cancel. I don't follow up or write to see how they're doing. I'm selfish that way.

It's a flaw I should work on, but I forget as well. It simply slips my mind until I come across something that reminds me of the person. Then I'll write to them, saying I'd been meaning to see how they're doing. They never believe me.

I don't mean to. I've just learned it's easier to live, *out of sight, out of mind* than *distance makes the heart grow fonder.*

My defense mechanism will kick in, making me forget about them before they forget about me. It's what happened when I lost people I loved at such a young age and realized anyone could abandon you in the split of a moment.

As the drops of water strengthen, I walk home. Tonight calls for warm coffee, my journal, and my soul. I've been itching to write. To release what I'm holding. I've been silenced for so long. Now that I've found my voice, I want to roar.

It's no longer enough to remain quiet when expected or to listen to others complain and not express my opinions. What I used to cower away from is now something I need to express. No more sitting idly. It's time to speak. Time to release the weight of these secrets.

My phone vibrates with an incoming message. I open the text from my mom.

Mom: I wonder what you were thinking about so deeply here

Attached is a photo of me. I look at it. I'm leaning over a stone railing looking out at the sea. Only a part of my face is visible, but it's clear my mind was deeper in thought than the bottom of the ocean my eyes were pretending to see.

Sometimes I wonder if my mom imagines what I could've been thinking about or really has no idea. I was a girl with too many deep thoughts for my age. It weighed me down, secluded me. I needed to break away from reality many times. They called me a daydreamer like it was a bad thing. Like it was a curse. I relished in daydreaming.

Even if at a young age I didn't understand it all, my soul was old for my body. It always has been. I still carried secrets that toppled me over. Made me crash. Made me terrified of the dark.

Time, like in this picture, where I could stare off somewhere without someone questioning what was bothering me, was what I craved then and still crave now. Seclusion that allows me time to lay out in front of my mind all the pieces that connect to me, so I can find a way to put them together where the jagged edges don't hurt. Where they aren't forced to be shoved into. I want flow when coming together in myself.

A sad smile creeps up on my face when I stop analyzing the photo. I write back, telling her I have no idea what I could've been thinking. She doesn't need to know the truth. It wouldn't do her any good. This is all mine. To heal and to own.

The person that needed to know for her personal healing already does. That removed a lot of the weight from me. It dissipated my possession over what happened.

I save the picture to my phone and open my journal. I ignore the rest of the messages coming in from my mom, making a mental note to respond to her later. Right now, I'm going to write.

❦

"Have you ever thought about approaching the person and saying what happened?" Matthias stares at me from across the toposcope at the top of Glastonbury Tor. I wanted to come back after I received that photo from my mom a few days ago.

"No." I shake my head. "He doesn't remember he did it. He was acting out of what was taught to him." I feel like I've explained this a million times. Or maybe it's what I've told myself to understand my situation better. My heart breaks for those that were hurt by people who truly meant to. I take in their pain so much, I forget that the little girl was also suffering because she didn't understand the bigger picture. For a long time, I lived wondering how he could look me in the eye knowing what had happened. He doesn't know. I'm not ready to remind him.

"Okay." He doesn't push.

"Have you ever thought about it?"

"No, but our situations are different. You know that. Mine was intentional. That's not as easy to forgive." His voice is tight.

I nod, understanding the hold that kind of pain has. It's holding me toward my grandfather, and he never touched me.

I stare out into the distance. The view clear compared to the first time we came. I watch the hills in the distance and trees lining patches of land. I inhale fresh air and exhale toxic thoughts.

"Stay with me tonight. The night will be clear, and the stars will be traveling across the sky."

I smile at Matthias. "Okay."

He walks around the toposcope and stands behind me, his arms wrapping around me and his chin resting on my shoulder.

I don't deserve him if I haven't forgiven.

The thought tenses my body. Is that true? Do I need to completely figure myself out before I can have Matthias in my life?

I shake the doubt away. We're supposed to continue growing, even if we are together.

But something in my gut kicks me.

Matthias sets a blanket outside of his house. The night is darker here in the countryside. My eyes take some time to adjust, and then I see Matthias's face looking at me. I lie back and stare up at the sky, reaching my hand out to him so he follows. The thought from earlier today has been stuck in my mind, and I'm trying with all my might to shake it away. Being extra attentive, extra touchy.

I curl into him when he's beside me on his back. We're silent at first, staring at the sky and hoping to see a shooting star or two. Some to make wishes on. A way to ask the cosmos to help fix the damage we're living. Or maybe to settle my mind. I know myself, it's only a matter of time before I destroy this..

Desperate to break that pattern, I move so I'm on top of Matthias and kiss him wildly. He jolts in surprise and then holds me to him as he allows my mouth to hopelessly connect with his.

Sensing my chaotic emotions, he stops me. "Navia."

"What?" My eyes widen.

"Slow down. Let's enjoy the night. We'll have time for that."

I move my body over his, feeling the bulge beneath me.

"I need it." My voice trembles.

"What's going on?" He stills my hips, the valleys between his eyebrows deeper than the Grand Canyon.

"Do you ever think we met before we were supposed to?" I voice my concern.

"No. Why do you ask?"

"Maybe we met before fate had planned. I've got so many emotions stirred, not done healing, that I think I saw you by accident. I don't deserve you if I'm still holding on to the past. I was doing good before then."

"Navia, slow down. If we weren't meant to meet, one of us wouldn't have been at that pub. We aren't supposed to have it all figured out. If we did, we'd be living in a different dimension. We came together to grow and heal. We came to provide the mirror the other needs. Our essence is connected and our energy beats together. When I look at you, I see things I'm fighting in myself. Our union isn't supposed to be easy. We reflect things in each other that will bring out pain, so we can finally let it go."

What he says makes sense. I know the truth in it, but my mind is attempting to overpower it. My self-worth is trying to diminish the feeling of deserving all of this. Matthias, my new home, my healing. It's an anchor that has rooted itself on the beaches of South Florida, giving just enough of its rope until I was happy. The instant tug surprised me, pulling me back, slowly dragging me into old ways and patterns, my hands not able to dig into the drowning water.

"I know," I whisper. It's half truth, half lie. I don't know if I have enough will to cut the ropes of the anchor while still swimming forward toward a life with Matthias.

"Love, look at me." I find his eyes in the night. He's always a light in the dark. "We're on track."

"I get it, but I feel anxious energy intersecting that belief."

"Let it go," he murmurs into my lips before he breathes into me. I greedily take his kiss, swallow it to save for another day.

His hands rest on my lower back. "Look at the stars. They're bright despite the distance. You and I knew each other once, long ago, amongst those stars. We met here because we were supposed to. If not, we'd still be living amongst those burning rocks."

I remain silent, allowing his words to wrap around me in a blanket of false confidence.

13
one lie

I used to have an impenetrable exterior. Lacquer was protecting my skin, my aura, my heart. People in my life haven't seen me cry in years. Whether because of a death, a new life, or simple human emotions. I used to take pride in it. I don't anymore. My turtle shell has done more harm than good. For myself anyway, others have gotten used to it. My metaphorical shell has become a part of my outfit—a dual purpose for protection and hiding. I'm a runner, as I've mentioned. So, when I flee, I go inside of myself. I suck in my breath until I'm stuck in a hole so far deep, I forget there's life outside of it. I lose my way back to the sunshine. It's been most of my life, so I didn't realize the negative effects until I began looking at myself. Really staring at my eyes in a mirror and seeing what was deeper. What caused the hiding, the running.

Something in my life must've fucked with my confidence in a confrontation. I can't remember what it is, and that's something I'll still need to work on. It impacted me. Maybe it was not being able to speak up when I was a little girl. I hid within instead, hid so others' hands couldn't find me or touch me. Maybe it was when I lost my paternal grandfather, and I learned people you love leave. So I'll leave before you do.

So many maybes are taken into account for this. And they can all add up to one response. Fractions of a whole that scarred me. When we're young, we're impressionable.

We don't have the understanding adults do. We don't process the same.

It's taken me a long fucking time to dig up that girl and remember glimpses of her. Not all fossils lie in the dirt. She was so happy and funny, and my god, was she strong, too. No one messed with her. Everyone wanted to follow her. My little girl was a leader, but at some point, I became a follower. I put dreams aside and I let fear guide me. I know what it's like to not believe in God and what it's like to hate the world. Betrayal runs deep, and trust issues are my foundation. But I got to a point where I'd had enough. The more I remembered the girl, the more I wanted the adult to be like her. I began to heal.

When I started working on my emotional health, my mental health, I realized things about myself I didn't want to see, let alone admit to someone. I also learned that I'm more than anger and worthlessness.

It's easy for me to fall into depression, get buried in a black hole found in that impenetrable shell. It's scary how easily I can want to end my life—choose death over living because quitting hurts less.

It doesn't though.

The pain of quitting is different. In its facility, we gain a complication in another part of ourselves. When we give up on ourselves, we hurt our soul. I've done that. I've turned my back on myself. I've damaged my body in unhealthy forms. Ruined my mind in what felt beyond repair.

But sometimes, the light seeps in even against the hardest exteriors. Sometimes, we find glimmers of hope and cling on to them, because although we're broken, we want to believe in something greater than our broken pieces.

It took me years to get to the point where I wasn't ashamed of showing my emotions. Years of sucking in my feelings when I was supposed to be vulnerable. When I was in a circle of trust.

But, I didn't believe in trust back then.

I do now.

I understand vulnerability isn't a weakness. Shells are supposed to have cracks. And living takes more courage than anything else we do.

But today, I've felt myself hiding. After the anxiety I felt with Matthias the other night, my mind has been spinning—convincing me that I can't have a happy life with him if mine isn't perfect.

I remind myself that there is no perfect. We're humans, living and learning. We can become isolated and miss some of the lessons that come with living with a companion. I want to choose Matthias, I do. But something inside of me is buzzing, daring me to go in the opposite direction. Something is telling me I haven't earned his affection yet. I need to fight harder to make myself worthy of his love. It's all in my mind, the ego whispering I'm not good enough . . . yet.

The vibrations on the wooden table call to me like a tempting drug. Matthias's name lights up my dark screen. I watch it, waiting for him to hang up. It's the third time he calls me. I've yet to answer. Instead, I'm staring ahead, wondering if this relationship with him is real. How much of it is just part of the initial excitement of meeting? An illusion?

How long will it take for him to leave me?

Like my dad's dad. My cousin. My first love. My second love. Like I did. Like I turned my back on my own self. How long before Matthias does the same?

This is why love is falsehood I refused to believe in.

You've worked hard to overcome that.

Internally, I know what is right for me and what isn't. Deep in my core, I know that my mind is playing with me. On the surface, I'm too blind by fear to notice it. I can't grasp my reality.

My body jumps when a hard knock echoes around my apartment. I remain still until a second one reverberates off the walls. I stand and look through the peephole, seeing Matthias running his hand through his hair. I open, a fake smile not even willing to appear.

"I've been calling your mobile." He walks into my home.

"I know."

"What's wrong? Why didn't you answer?" He tugs his hair as he brushes it with his fingers, pacing the living room.

"I don't know. I was thinking." *Fleeing.*

"What about?" He stops his incessant roaming and looks me dead in the eyes. Eyes I want to memorize. Color blue as a setting sky, a hint of dusk in them.

"My worth." No sense in lying. He'll just know.

His eyebrows scrunch as his eyes squint to look at me. I'm still in my pajamas, and I'm sure the mess of my hair is knotted in its bun. "What about it?"

"I'm not done working on myself," I state.

"Okay? That's life. We've got continuous lessons to learn and work through. It's part of being alive."

"I know," I whisper.

"So then?"

I inhale. "I don't deserve to be with you when I'm holding on to so much bullshit from the past. When I'm not allowing myself to find forgiveness in my heart. If I can't let it go, then karma will just take you away from me. It's as if my life isn't ready to receive you. I didn't even really believe in this kind of love until I saw you. Thought it was all in my head, a daydreamer's made up reality based on romance novels she gets lost in because they're easier than real life."

He's speechless as he looks at me.

"I know we both have things to work through. I know meeting has resurfaced a lot of pain," I try to defend before he speaks. "But I need to get my things straightened out before I can give someone more of myself."

Matthias walks toward me, stopping three inches in front of me. I calculate the actual distance, looking down at our feet, as his silence swirls me up in its blanket of uncertainty and hurt. When I dare look up at his face, my words are etched on his skin, marking its beauty with pain.

My doing.

His hurt is my doing.

Another person I push. Will he be willing to pull?

This isn't normal. My reaction to intimate relationships isn't healthy. I'm a lightning bolt to those that care about me. I strike when you least expect it. I draw you in only to burn you.

Matthias is still looking at me, wordless. He walks around me, my skin crawling with the lingering of his gaze and his silence seeping into my pores.

He grabs a book. The same one he's been reading. He holds it in the air, facing me. "You're acting like her, like Samantha. You're using her mask to hide behind. Her cynicism. You're stuck in fiction instead of living in reality. You think you need to be this *strong* character when in reality it's your weakness shining through. You aren't Samantha, but I can't convince you of that. You've got to believe it for yourself. I don't need to finish reading this book to know how it ends. But I'm not Max, either." Tears drip from my eyes as I hear his words.

"You lie when you say you don't want love. Don't need

it. When you say love in fiction is easier. I see it in you—the desire to be wanted, the desire to have a companion. You're quick to be honest with others, but you lie to yourself. You pretend your independence is all you need. You need more, I feel it in your pulse and in your breath when it hitches before I touch you. I feel it in your energy when you look away because the moment is too intense, too intimate." He steps closer again.

"You want this. You want someone who can keep you safe while allowing you to run wild. You want someone to drive four hundred miles with you in the middle of the night because there is a meteor shower that won't occur again for another hundred years. Look at me. Being in love doesn't make you vulnerable, it makes you brave. Hiding behind these," he holds the book in my face. "That makes you weak." He slings the book on the couch.

"I'm not giving up on us. I'm not giving up on you. I'm giving you a chance to catch up and realize what I'm saying is true." He kisses my cheek and walks around me. I turn around, watching his body move farther from me.

I stand, numb and cold. Is Matthias right? Of course, he is. I'm a walking contradiction of emotions and voids because I will not acknowledge all of my truths. I know most of them, but I hide behind that one lie to the extreme that it prevents me from fully experiencing life.

His words echo in my mind. *You aren't Samantha.* So many times I counted her and me as the same person. She has so much of me, maybe pieces he's yet to discover.

Impulsive.

That's always been me. Jump the gun on anything because my body reacts faster than my mind can process. Except for when it counts. Like right now. When I should be acting instead of staying rooted like a heavy tree.

I watch him walk away, his shoulders tight with tension. My lack of reaction is maddening. I want to yell and tell him he's wrong. I want to ask him to stop walking, but I can't. I've never seen him angry, and that alone creates a whirl of fear storming inside my stomach, threatening to destroy the inner peace I've grown to carry within. A burst of truth thrown at me.

I jolt at the sound of a slamming door.

I lumber to the chair in the corner of my living room. Dazed, I stare at the void in this room which reflects that in my heart.

I came here for an adventure, my wanderlust soul seeking something *more*. I didn't expect to find my *him,* though I secretly knew I would. I was too independent to admit it out loud, too stubborn, but somewhere deep I hoped he'd be here. I hoped he'd be the man I always imagined he was, and he exceeded that. *And I let him walk away*. With my heart. With my happiness.

I place my head in my hands and gasp for air. If he leaves forever, I lose my forever. I lose everything I aspired to become, my purpose. We were a team. *Are* a team.

I press the heel of my hand over my chest, pushing hard to ease the pain. A building pressure that threatens my sanity feeds my shadow and starves my light until I'm swirling uncontrollably in an unwinding spiral.

Can a love like ours reach a limit? Expire into an abyss? I thought when I found him, I'd be liberated of the traps that steer me away from love. I thought we'd dance flawlessly into the night, knowing we had an eternity to make up for. I thought when I was united with my twin flame, it'd all click.

Foolish.

Nothing is easy in love. A soulmate doesn't facilitate the

process, let alone a twin flame. I should've known this, but I was blinded by his eyes and smile. I was blinded by the reality of having him in front of me. It was exhilarating to be with him, moving forward on the same path. We had it all.

No amount of pressure will alleviate this pain from my chest. Again, my ego interfered with my heart. A lesson I can't get behind because I don't know where it starts and ends.

Where Matthias and I start and end.

I don't know where to go from here.

14
stale coffee & heartache

The same mug, full of coffee, sits on the table from the night Matthias slammed the door on his exit. *I'm not giving up on us.*

I've replayed his words, nonstop, for the last week. I've had to reschedule my appointments. I can't help others when my energy is a black cloak that wraps anyone who gets near me. It wouldn't be fair to take money from my clients when I'm not giving them the best service I'm capable of. Makenna didn't question me, but she knows this is all caused by heartbreak. I could tell by the way she told me to sort what was in my heart.

I scratch my head as I wander around the space in my apartment. I've barely slept the last two days, asking myself what the fuck happened. How did I push Matthias away? Better yet, why?

At one point in my life, I did express love. I would tell people how I felt. I stopped using the phrase, *I love you.* I shiver just having to think it. I've turned so cynical when it comes to love, not only with an intimate partner but with family and friends. The belief that if I love you, you'll leave became so ingrained in me from a young age.

I've seen the artwork I did in school as a little girl for my mom telling her I love her. I can't tell her those words anymore. I don't feel them. It's as if when it comes to love, a void was scraped out of me. A hollow space where nothing grows.

And the older I get, and the more I see what people

who are supposed to love you did, the void expands like a black hole threatening to swallow a galaxy.

I stalk to my room and open the armoire. I dig through a bag that holds my scrapbooks, sifting through each one until I find the page I'm looking for. I'd forgotten I made this page until I packed my things to move here. I almost threw it away when I found it.

The dark beige paper gives this scrapbook page a distressed look. The sepia photo adds to the vintage style. And the damn poem I wrote about The Saint in Red before I knew of his sins taunts me. I search for scotch tape and tear a piece. Then, I walk into my living room and tape the paper to the wall at eye level.

I stare at his photo. His buzz cut, the smirk on his profile, it all mocks me. I pace in circles, hands on my hips until I face him head-on. My palm makes contact with the photo. The sting ripples through my skin, but it doesn't stop me from hitting his face again. I slap it over and over again until the picture begins to wrinkle.

When I can't handle the pain in my hand anymore, I step back, my pained hand coming up to cover my mouth and sobs move through me. I stare at his face.

"You fucked this all up. You," I point at him. "You created this pattern for all of us to steal, weaved it into our DNA. You ruined us all. You were the catalyst, you evil, evil man. They say that everyone acts on their own past. You weren't supposed to bring the pain, though. You were supposed to protect us. You were the example we all lived by. What a fucking despicable example you gave us. Abuse. Torment. Disgust. You're a disgust. That's what you are." Tears fall as the anger spins out of control.

I tear the poem and read it aloud. A copy of the same one that taunted me not too long ago. The Spanish praise for a false man tears at my heart. I wrote these word with such meaning after he passed as a tribute to him. I ball the paper up in my hand and spit on it. Then, I tear it into shreds. Once the pieces are torn, I ball them up again. Now the words that were used to make him a hero are nothing. That feeling I had for him at fifteen no longer exists. It died when his image was ruptured, the truth of the man he was spilling from it.

"You caused a ripple effect on us. You damaged us, tainted us with labels we'll always carry. You abused your children. God. What kind of sick bastard were you? Your actions led for the rest of us to be harmed by others. Were you ever even able to love? To care about someone else but yourself? Motherfucker." My words spit from my mouth without a second thought. I'm not even fully aware of everything I'm telling him.

"Didn't you know the consequences your actions would have? Did you care? You're a sick fuck," I hiccup.

I fall to the ground as if my spine has turned to jelly. Crumbled, and in a way, it has. My backbone has been weak since I found out the truth. I lie on the tile, my back pressed against the hard surface, and stare at the light in the ceiling.

I wish I could erase him completely, but I know that's not possible. Whether I want to or not, he's a part of my history, my ancestor. I've learned too much about our family lineage, the energy we carry, the way they influence our DNA, to think I could just pretend I don't carry his blood in me.

It's scary to think you come from someone who could hurt children to such an extent. Wrapping my head around that is hard. It makes me wonder if any of us could be like him. Do we inherit the need to abuse? To feel pleasure from a child? So many questions whirl around.

Patterns.

I want to break them, free us from them. This energy carried amongst generations, how many before him were the same?

Our family is tainted by the heartache of knowing people who are supposed to protect you, damage you.

I pushed Matthias away because of that.

My nails try to dig into the tile as if it were dirt. My fingers burn against the floor from my attempt.

I continue to stare at the ceiling as I think how this pattern has affected me beyond what I lived as a little girl.

It was in more aspects of my life beyond that. I know what it's like to live with someone harassing you, making you feel afraid. I've lived in fear. We have a family friend that would hit on me, and feared that one day he'd get drunk and go through with the words he'd say. I became so distant, to hide so nothing would happen. Why did I have to live in silence?

My mother once asked if I had said or done something at some point to give him the impression that something could happen between us. I answered with a firm no, upset she'd think that. It took some time to forgive her, but then again, she was also conditioned to believe women were at fault for taunting men. When this friend came to live with us for some time, I would sleep with my door locked . . . *just in case*.

I've lived with that fear. What was a joke to him was my cruel reality. Just because he was a friend, he could say things that made me feel uncomfortable. To this day, I keep my distance.

Why is it that I attract people like that? Is it because of the abuse? Do I carry a sign that reads, *I'm only good for my body*? Could it be because that's what I believe I'm good for?

I've set myself up for situations like that, never feeling worthy of someone digging deeper than my pussy.

Or is it because I think someone will only love me for my body when all I want is to be loved for my soul?

I'm still thinking about my actions of a week and a half ago with Matthias. I threw my body at him, instinctively doing exactly what I question is wrong with me.

Matthias isn't a scumbag or an asshole trying to overpower someone any way he can. He is freedom and sunshine and warmth. He's a burning star, galaxies away that makes the view on this earth a little more beautiful.

And I tried to throw my body at him, knowing he's the one person who wants and values my soul just as much. My insecurities are swirling, the ego showing itself.

The following days from the night at Matthias's house have been filled with shame. It led to him leaving me alone in this space, with my head exploding with thoughts that are dragging me down.

I sit up and stare at the paper taped to the wall. Standing, I run my palms down my thighs and rip the paper from its holding place. I tear it up like I did the poem.

No more.

No more pain.

No more shame.

No more control.

No more patterns.

This ends now.

With me, standing here.

What he did to our family will no longer occur. I may not be tearing apart his role in our family because he came before me, therefore, without him, I wouldn't exist. I'm tearing up the energy surrounding his actions. The taboo. The blind eye we've all turned. No more lies. Only truths.

It's time I take action instead of carrying this secret with me. I may have been more open about it, but it's still not out in the open. I'm still hiding a part of it, and in order to have full freedom, I need to be honest.

The thought alone scares me. To face it. To say it. To hurt someone in the process. Maybe instead of hurt, it will be freedom. I can't judge it. Not anymore. Not if I want to heal.

I'll need Makenna's help in releasing this.

15
inner-child

I'm not a religious person. I stopped going to church long ago when I felt the hypocrisy of the people attending fill the air. One time, a family of four was sitting a few rows in front of me. They were talking, drinking soda, and eating chips. As much as I tried to, I couldn't look away. I condemned them though it wasn't in my right.

My mom would try to get me to go to church with her on Mother's Day or Christmas after I told her I'd no longer be attending. *That's the only gift I want,* she'd say. For me to attend church. It was manipulative. She eventually stopped. I've forgiven a lot of the manipulations she used to throw my way. It's eye-opening when you realize the resentment you're holding isn't hurting anyone but yourself.

So I released the suppressed anger her actions and words would cause. I freed myself of them. It took years. I never thought her and I would reach a point where I'd call her just to talk. Just to know how her day is going. I was too proud. Too hurt. Too frustrated.

It took understanding her to release the bitterness I was braiding between us. With releasing, it's almost as if you forget the weight you were carrying. I may remember how her manipulations would make me feel, but in forgiveness, I've found a sense of peace that heals the battle wounds.

I think of her as I stare up at the church before me. I may not be a religious person, yet this is where I landed in search of guidance.

I walk in, feeling the cold stone beneath my hands. People always focus on stained glass as if it were the most magnificent thing. For me, it's the stonework of the architecture, the true art. The etching and carving, creating foundations out of stone so hard, it'd shatter our bones.

I enter the building, finding a pew not too far from the altar. I bow my head, hands folded, as I walk. *Some habits are hard to break.* When I'm happy with the location of my seat, I drop onto my knees, hitting the cushioned kneelers, and fold my hands on the pew in front of me.

So many thoughts cloud my mind. None offering clarity or allowing me to focus on what I came in here for. The desolation I felt when Matthias walked out of my apartment has consumed me.

Why must I ruin the good stuff? It's a conundrum I can't shake, even when I know it will hurt me in the end.

The wounds are my muse.

It's almost as if without the pain I don't think I can move forward in life, as if pain feeds my drive, my creativity.

I have become a captive of the sadness, the darkness, the shadows that linger, lying to themselves that they want to find the light. It imprisons me. The pain clips my wings when I'm meant to soar amongst the stars. The awe-striking nebulas that prove there's so much more to life than the superficial—go to school, get a college degree, be married and a mother by twenty-five, work until you retire, and then die.

I want to receive death proud of my life, having loved, and lived wildly. I don't want to lie in a bed, before my last breath, and regret. I don't want to arrive at death holding onto hatred.

I stare up at the altar, at the statue of Christ suffering on a cross. Why show us his pain and then preach about the good his sacrifice did? The image will stay with us longer than your fleeting words about unconditional love.

Jesus, I surrender. No more pain. No more hatred. No more thinking I don't deserve love. Can I have a love like Matthias's while I still walk this life as a sinner? While I continue to condemn other sinners.

I rub my eyes and suck in a breath.

I want to accept love. I want to release pain. I want to understand that I can be happy without guilt. This is more than my relationship with Matthias, this is about my life. I surrender. I want to be free of this baggage, of this belief that . . .

I sigh, gulping for air.

I deserve better than my own torture and punishments. I deserve to live a full life. I choose life.

I stand from my kneeling position, feeling more confident about where I'm going and what I'm doing. Makenna asked me this morning why I rejected my inner-child so much, why I was so angry with my little girl.

I stared at her, blinked twice, and lied. I told her I wasn't angry. I didn't reject her. I told her I've been wanting to embrace her, pull her back into my life so I can be the strong little girl again, regain the bravery I lost with age.

It was a lie.

I rejected her spark when my freedom was stolen from me. I resented her for having to keep quiet. I dulled her so no one else would look at her and want a piece of her.

She failed me. But it's not fair to throw that all on her. To blame her. She did what she could to protect me. She tried to move forward the best way she could while remaining safe.

Our psyche is an interesting thing. It holds our reality but also masks the pain so as not to obstruct our life path. However, that kind of self-preservation ruins it. Had I admitted all this to myself, maybe I could have a healthy relationship with another person. I could have asked Matthias to stay instead of letting him walk away. I wouldn't be leaving an empty church on a rainy, spring day, searching for some kind of answer from the divine, an answer I should be able to find within me.

I head home to do the *homework* Makenna assigned— meditate with my inner-child and find forgiveness. The thought alone opens up to a million excuses of things I need to do that are more important than that. Anything that won't add to my already somber mood and broken heart. All I've done in the last few days is repeat Matthias's exit from my apartment and from my life. He hasn't written, and I haven't called.

But I hold on to the hope that he really isn't giving up on us. Because up until this point in my life, people have left. They've moved, died, found someone else. I pushed Matthias. He saw the warning signs though I wasn't even aware of them. He felt the shutting down before I pressed the button to self-destruct. He read my words and understood how I hide behind them, creating false aspects of myself. He was wrong about one thing—in a way, I am Samantha. I wrote her based on me, on the part of me I have released. I grew the same way she did and maybe because of that, I feared he would be my Max.

Their story isn't mine despite the similarities I painted on Samantha, like a well-worn canvas I marked with my strokes. This is my story. It's ours. It's different.

He's not giving up on us.

Our purpose in each other's lives is different.

I climb the stairs to my apartment and enter my home, the chilly silence slicing my skin.

I burn incense while I mentally prepare myself. Then, I

sit back on the couch and search for soothing music to stop the race in my mind from sprinting faster than it already is.

I press play on a song and close my eyes, focusing on my breath and the bells that ring in the music.

If I could just clear my head and connect with that aspect of myself, I can work through this. *Just breathe.* I picture myself as a child, smiling and happy.

My eyes tightly squeeze when I see myself like that. A slight shake of my head keeps me distracted.

Fuck.

My mind is overpowering my soul. I throw my head back and puff out air through my mouth. I relax my body, remaining motionless as soft music fills my ears and woodsy smoke fills my nose.

Don't picture her as anything, just connect with yourself.

I stare at the wall ahead of me until my vision blurs and my eyes close. I relax further, sinking into the couch cushions. Colors fill the space behind my eyelids until I'm somewhere between the present moment and a place so deep inside me I begin to see motion inside of myself, flashes of images and people's faces. I allow them to pull me in, take me to a place that will provide some answers, provide healing.

Excuse me, excuse me, excuse me. There you are. I hear a breathless voice that matches a disheveled girl—no more than seven. Her stringy hair is a mess, and her porcelain skin contrasts her black outfit. Her face is relieved as she looks at me, as if she's been running around looking for me and her lungs were giving out on her. I wait for her to say more, but my body jolts and my mind returns to the surrounding space. I lose that girl, but her image is so clear in my mind.

She looked like a mess.

I smile. So many times I was that mess as a child. Hell,

as an adult. I run a hand through my knotted curls before tossing my hair in a bun.

Who was that girl? She looked nothing like me, yet she felt like me. She was searching for me, and I've been hiding.

I stretch my arms over my head as I lean my head side to side, stretching my neck. I can't get over the expression the girl showed. I start and head out to the balcony, shutting the music on my phone on the way out. I sneak out into the warm afternoon, enjoying the breeze that swipes over my skin. I lean over the railing, looking down at the gardens I love. The flowers are blooming, yet I've stayed stagnant.

I allow myself a few seconds to wonder how Matthias is doing before shutting that down and returning to the work Makenna told me to do. Closing my eyes, I try to go back to that girl, find her, let her know I'm done running. No more pretending I'm peachy.

One evening I was talking to a friend. Mid-conversation, she interrupted me with a heavy-loaded question. One I wasn't prepared for. One I thought I had hidden so well.

"Were you molested as a child?"

As soon as her words processed, I froze. She must've noticed because she immediately apologized and told me I didn't have to answer if I wasn't comfortable. But she already knew the answer, that's why she asked.

I told her it was okay. Then, I realized this was a learning moment for me—continue to hide or speak my truth.

I decided to speak.

I told her how only one other person knew, who had helped me sort through the emotions to heal them, how I felt no grievance toward the person, how it hurt more to hold the secret than what I lived.

Her question had stopped me in my tracks for one reason. All those masks I thought were so securely tightened around my being, that I trusted, were flawed. Holes punctured them that allowed my truth to slip through them for those who were really paying attention.

I learned at that moment that we can never really hide who we are. We put so much energy into becoming something else, something less painful when everything we are has always penetrated those walls.

For the past few years, I've been working on removing masks, shedding what isn't mine—things I took ownership of without permission. I lost parts of me in covering up.

I lost my little girl, lost my essence, lost my way. But since that conversation, I've told two more people, all to help them become free of their own ties.

Maybe I'm just working too hard on helping others because I've failed myself. I haven't helped myself, so it's easier to improve the outside world than the inside universe that moves in me.

I need to help myself.

I walk back inside and head straight for my room. Spying my current journal on my nightstand, I grab it and the pen hooked on the pages. I return to the balcony to watch the descending sun and write a letter that is long overdue.

16
i forgive me

Dear Navia,

I don't know where to begin. This all sounded so much easier in my head than it really is. Write a letter to myself. I feel weird. Like I'm talking, writing, to me when I can just think it in my head. I guess that's the purpose though, to remove the head and just express what I feel.

What do I feel?

Sometimes, it's an emptiness that consumes me. As if I'm alone in this world, trying to figure out how to swim upstream when I have hundreds of hands on the shore willing to help me. I'm blind to them. Blind to the help because I think I live easier with the struggle, it seems to fuel me. Maybe I'm afraid to heal completely because I don't know what will be of my life then. They say when you treat one aspect another pops up, so you can slowly release it all until you're truly free of karma and ego.

I'm babbling on paper. Would that be pappling? Ugh, sorry. Bad joke. You should know by now I make awkward and stupid jokes when I'm nervous or unsure. You are me, after all.

I take a deep breath and refocus, trying to release the

nerves that are causing pointless chatter in my head. Inhale. Exhale. My body relaxes, muscles turning soft.

I'm sorry if I let you down. I'm sorry if you feel as if I've abandoned you. As if I threw everything you are to a side and tossed things I don't need over you, to hide you, like a hoarder. I may not hoard physical things, but I hoard emotions.

I didn't even realize what I was doing until I woke up one day and noticed I was different. I was no longer the carefree, courageous girl I used to be. Instead, I would hide. I would hate to be left alone. I needed lights on because the darkness terrified me. Sometimes it still does. Not only children can be afraid of the dark.

But in giving in to each fear, I gave away the strength I used to carry. The strength I didn't even know adults admired. I gave away you. Me.

I feel like I've lost so much time of my life not being who I was born to be. Focusing on the shit and disappointment. Confusion took the place of strength, and I cowered at the idea of shining, of allowing someone else to see me. I devalued myself. I made myself believe I was unworthy of love. Didn't need it. Love was a false fairytale they fed me to make me believe in something. But as a child, I connected love to leaving, to pain, to abandonment.

I used to joke by saying I had abandonment and commitment issues. It was easier to throw that out at people as a joke than have to seriously express it. To this day, I still have those fears. I still believe that love will lead to loneliness. And I did just that with Matthias. I did that with you. I abandoned you instead of proving that not everyone leaves. How could I when my own self couldn't show up for myself.

I'm sorry.

I'm sorry I allowed years of pain to win over love. I'm sorry I shut you down, silencing your voice because I was too consumed with how bad people were. I was too shocked to speak up. Too embarrassed. It was so embarrassing to have to admit what I had lived through. It still kinda is. For that, I apologize because you deserve better than someone who turns her back on herself.

You were just a girl.

You should've been laughing and running around, free. Not suddenly terrified of being left alone without supervision.

I want you to know that it's okay to feel sad. It's okay to cry, it's okay just to feel. But I also want you to know that you're strong. You are worth so much. I love you.

From now on, I will show you that. I will love myself and care for who I am, showing my truth. I will go back to my essence and live from that place. I will release hatred toward those who wronged me directly and indirectly. The only way to be honest is by embracing all of me, flaws and perfections. I will no longer be ashamed of my story or how I reacted to it. It's time to break the silence. It's time to heal. It's time to forgive.

So, I'm sorry.

For not being present. For hiding you and burying you so deep, I don't even remember who you are. Who I am.

I'm working on it though. I'm trying hard to release fear and find that spark of life I used to have.

What I really should apologize for is letting you get hurt. I should've protected you better, been more aware. I'm sorry I let you down. I'm sorry for allowing someone to touch you when you didn't want it. I'm so sorry.

You were just a girl with dreams and so much joy. With a bright light that was dimmed. I had the key to it all, but I let the light die away instead of finding a way to keep it going, a way to rise above.

I know I can't continue to carry the blame. I can't hold on to other people's pain either. I'm not some kind of chest that is here to pile on more and more. It's the curse of an empath though. We take it on, willingly or unwillingly.

I should've just been more focused on you. On me. All these years. I could've done more to get to this place than I have. It's taken too long.

I can't judge that now and let it weigh me down because then this letter is pointless. I have to focus that I'm now taking the time to heal this part of me. It's weird, writing a letter to myself and speaking as if it's someone else, but in a way it is. I'm speaking to me, the one that was real. From a point that is more an illusion, a falsehood.

When I have a little girl, I'll make sure to show her the magic of this world despite ugliness existing. I'll be the strong leader. Starting today. I am a strong leader. I am courageous. I am safe.

Thank you for not giving up on me. For shining every bit you could, so I'd remember and crave to go back to that person. Thank you for your innocence, though it was stripped from you. Thank you for loving the wildflowers. For reminding me how to play.

We're going to be more than okay. I promise to spend more time connected to the life I'm living and less time disconnected from myself. I promise to go back to the beginning, to reach for your hand and incorporate you to what I'm living. I promise to forgive myself for the harm I did to myself. For the times I didn't choose life because it was easier to quit. From now on, I choose to live. I choose to experience it all because I want to and no longer hide from things because I'm afraid that patterns will repeat themselves.

It's time to go back to my core.

Love,

Navia

P.S. Because I always forget to add something in. What happened isn't our fault. We don't need to drown in it. We have the choice to be free.

17
the keeper of secrets

I turn in bed, shoulders tight from sleep, and notice the sun is just starting to rise. As soon as I stand, the folded chunk of paper filled with words catches my eye under the purple amethyst. I sigh as the emotional waves come back to me like a dizzying hangover. My exhale travels through me until it escapes my parted lips.

Writing that letter was a good release; however, it resurfaced a lot more than I had originally considered. It focused on parts I hadn't paid attention to when I became poisoned with the stories I learned as an adult. Another thing to cover up my truth, who I am at my core. It also reminded me of the person I lost because of all I've been holding.

I move through my home until I make it out on the balcony. I shiver, wrapping my arms around my body, and squint my eyes at the change in lighting. The strong sphere of fire shines its rays through the trees. My right foot steps on my left one as I lean back into the wall. The chilled concrete wakes me up as goosebumps cover my skin, but the view is worth the cold morning.

"Thank you." A whispered prayer. "Another day to make things right." I inhale shakily, tears blurring the rays I'm admiring.

I came here for great things, part of it being my own healing. I hadn't expected that to knock me down so hard, so fast. I thought my own healing would continue in a static progression where I could take my time, not a sudden strike of immense emotional baggage. I guess that's the thing when we take action into our own lives, the Universe accelerates everything around us. *Ready or not.*

I rub my eyes as the sun continues to rise, lighting up the sky and my surroundings, brightening up the flowers below me. I love moments like this where I take the time to pause and be present. It's not often I do this, as much as I want to. But how can I not pause with the beauty around me? My body trembles from the cold, my tank top and shorts not ideal to be standing out here in the early morning.

Time for coffee.

I make my way into the kitchen to start the coffee and grab my journal and sweater while I wait for the coffee to brew.

My mind wanders to Matthias, wondering if he's sleeping or awake, watching the same sun as I was. Before I met him, I questioned if the person I ended up with would be good-hearted. If he would fool me the way my grandfather had. Would I be like my grandmother? Sleeping with the devil and not strong enough to protect the people I love.

I wondered if the victim would become the perpetrator and I'd marry him. Have children with him.

Then I saw his eyes. I knew, at that moment, everything his mouth wouldn't tell me. He wants better than what he had.

I want to believe that at least.

Except I let him walk. I wasn't any stronger than my grandmother because I disappointed the person I love. In an entirely different space than what she did, I also didn't stand my ground.

Her memory weighs heavy on my heart. How I wish I

could talk to her now, ask her questions. I don't hate her anymore. Although, there are still some things I can't comprehend.

I guess it's not for me to understand.

With my sweater keeping me warm and the coffee mug steaming, I go back out onto the balcony and take a seat this time, opening my journal to a new page.

The Keeper of Secrets

I add the date on the right side of the title and begin writing a new section for the book I'm working on. As soon as the title hit me, I began to release so much more. The writing took a different route than my original idea, but it's turning out much better than I could've imagined.

My thoughts are a bit scattered this morning after last night but writing this is the one thing that will center me, put me back on my path, so I can be the person Matthias deserves. Not a flighty woman that he'll never know will push or pull.

He deserves to have every part of me in true transparency, the same way I deserve his love and affection.

I should just call him.

I reach for my phone instead of my pen and toy with the idea of contacting him. My guilt stops me from pressing down on his name. Shame for showing him my weakness. Guilt for not going after him. Sadness because I know right now we need this time apart. Realizations like these are hard to embrace.

I can't continue to repeat these patterns, of turning around and ignoring the person that's standing in front of me. Twice in my young adult life, I ditched dates at school dances because their presence was too consuming, too suffocating. Instead of talking or just enjoying one night, I fled. It's what I'm good at—fleeing into the crowd to be swallowed up, camouflaged not to be found.

I turn my phone over, hiding the screen from my wandering eyes, and grab my pen again, prepared to continue working on the book that will help free me. Or at least, that will be a step in the direction of truly using my voice for a greater good.

The Keeper of Secrets

I begin to scribble on the page.

Though patterns repeat themselves in generations, they have a purpose. Similar experiences surface to show the family that healing needs to be done. These patterns are a way of calling attention. Many times they are overlooked, a shrug that he or she has similarities of a family member because they are family, after all. In reality, the person is begging for someone to pay attention, realize that something isn't right. Sometimes, someone does pay attention. They realize something has to be healed. Not just the person showing these "symptoms" but the family as a whole.

Breaking patterns down generational lineage is powerful for the current generation, those that came before, and those that will come after. Energetic freedom.

When it comes to secrets covered in families, the weight is heavier. Exclusion causes more energetic ties and tears.

I close my eyes. My family has all of these and more. Maybe it's why when I made the switch in this book the words began to flow. It's all so familiar. However, it's not just my family that has secrets, regrets, and pain. We all do, but not all may be aware. My hope with this book is to help others. Maybe tap the tip of the iceberg so that people begin to become conscious of how to release the baggage limiting their magic.

Shaking my head, I grimace when I drink cold coffee. Noting the time on my phone, I go inside and change. It's too pretty of a day to spend it indoors. I take advantage of my day off, more like prescribed staycation by Makenna so I can work through my emotions, and head into town. I'll stop by to see her later on and tell her about the progress I made yesterday.

As I make my way through the streets, the town still quiet, I walk into a small, quaint café for breakfast and fresh coffee.

As I wait to be served, I remember something I read in a book recently. I open my app and search my highlights for *In the Gray*. When I read this part, I had to stop and breathe. The truth hit me with force straight to my chest. I paused, tears falling down my face because those words were meant for me. The same way they can be meant for so many others who struggle to forgive themselves.

I re-read the words that touched me so many months ago.

"...you must forgive yourself. You must accept that no matter what you were wearing, what you did or didn't say, it's not your fault. Until you stop hating yourself for what happened to you, you won't be able to let someone else love you."

I close my eyes, trapping the tears threatening to embarrass me in public and catch my breath. A.D. McCammon wrote such real words in a tale of fiction. But that's just it, right? Fiction is always inspired by reality. How many people feel that way? Blaming and hating yourself because you didn't act. I know I do. I hate myself because it happened when I was a child and too weak to defend myself, paralyzed by fear. I hate that it shut down my passion for life, confusion stopping me from saying something was wrong because it would create so much shit in our family. What I didn't know is the shit was already dumped on us.

I smile at the waitress when she hands me my coffee and breakfast, pretending like everything is okay. *Another mask.* Sitting straighter, I thank her and decide I don't need to hide. Let her think I'm heartbroken. It's the damn truth.

I inhale the aroma swirling from my mug and blow the steaming liquid. These secrets killed me. Now I'm carrying secrets that belong to others, not mine to tell, yet I hold them in my hand. I can't speak for them, but maybe I can help them speak for themselves by being an example. I don't want to be the keeper of secrets anymore. I don't want to carry on more than I have. I want to be happy, truly…with Matthias.

I want to be free.

Instead of writing in my journal, I enjoy my breakfast, disconnecting from everything that isn't solely focused on me moving forward. Disconnecting from everything that isn't this present moment, my coffee, scrambled eggs, and toast. Right now, nothing else matters.

After finishing up, I walk out into the cool morning. I pause, debating if to go right or left when I stare straight ahead as movement captures my attention like a mesmerizing meteor shower. Blue eyes meet mine, sensing me across the way, and a soft smile marks his face as he nods once. His hand grips the top of the open car door before climbing in and driving away. I haven't seen him since he walked out of my apartment, but his presence will always calm me despite the way we left things.

I close my eyes and face the sky, memorizing his smile, directed at *me.* I decide to go back to Chalice Well.

Matthias was here. We can't seem to miss each other despite the current break in our course. My soul will always call to his, the same way it had before I met him.

⟡

I walk into the office where I find Makenna sitting on the sofa, reading a book.

"I've been waiting for you," she says without lifting her gaze from the book.

"I was writing." I sit across from her in the armchair, dropping the feather I found along the way into the bowl she leaves for me.

"Have you found a flow?" Makenna drops the book on the low table that separates us and stares at me.

"Yes. I have a title as well." I giggle when her eyebrows raise. "*The Keeper of Secrets.*"

"Interesting title," is her only comment before she pauses, fingers grazing her lips.

"Yeah," I draw out, waiting to see if she says something else.

"Why did you choose that?"

Choose? As if I could choose it. "It came to me," I explain.

"And why do you think that choice of words?"

I exhale, knowing what she's doing. She wants me to look for the answers within myself. "Because I'm tired of carrying everyone else's secrets, even secrets they don't know they have dug deep into the crevices of their souls. I'm tired of keeping my own hidden in the dark night, sharing them only with the moon and stars. It's time for people to understand the extremities of holding on. The damage it does and the years of pain that deteriorates our purpose. I'm tired, Makenna, so fucking tired of holding on to everyone's shit without being asked to. The keeper of secrets simply means that the chest that holds them can no longer survive. Eventually, it bursts open from too many piles of baggage. It's time for the truth to triumph. I hope this book heals to those who read it."

A small smile appears on Makenna's face. "My darling, if you write from the heart there's no way it won't offer healing."

"Why do I have to know so much?" I look down, choking on my words.

"Because someone has to be strong enough to bring them to light. How else will healing occur?"

I look up at her, a frown taking over. "It made me lose Matthias."

She shakes her head. "You can't lose someone like Matthias. Soul connections are impossible to cut. You took time, both of you, to deal with your own challenges. He gave you the space he felt you needed. He's allowing you time to heal for yourself, not for him or your relationship, because he understands that when you do, it will also provide healing for your relationship. When you're in balance, everything around you will be as well."

I wipe my cheek with the back of my thumb and nod. "How long do I have to wait?"

"Dear, that choice is up to you." She smiles. "How long do you want the poison of anger and resentment in your system?"

"No more," I shake my head as I whisper.

"Forgive yourself. It's the only way you'll be able to forgive others."

I think back to the quote I read while eating breakfast and the letter I wrote to myself. I tell Makenna about it.

"Burn the letter. Let the fire transmute it so you can be free of it and return the ashes to the Earth." I nod, listening to her instructions. "You don't need to hold on to that anymore. When we accept forgiveness, it's done. Why clasp on to it? It's done. That's it." She swipes her hands together.

She makes it sound so easy, yet there's truth to her words. We hold on from the ego, feeling as if we need a certain amount of time to process emotions when in reality time is irrelevant in the universe. Time is manmade. If we're moving forward at an unimaginable speed, then what I forgave should be done with, released. My mind is what continues to play the pain on a loop. My soul has already forgiven.

My soul has already forgiven, I repeat to myself. *I've already forgiven.*

I shiver as I repeat the mantra, my eyes closing for a beat longer than a normal blink. It's time to release the role of secret keeper and live for myself.

18
universal undoing

It's amazing how as soon as you make a choice that is for your highest good it manifests. When I decided I was no longer living for others or in the protection of others, I saw the shift, free of time limitations or deadlines. Quickly, too.

After I left Makenna yesterday, I went home and burned the letter, placing the ashes on the soil in the garden below my apartment. Talking to her and writing as self-expression instead of forced words of how I think they *should* be released a huge weight.

When we become open, aware, and trusting, the universe unstitches, thread by thread, the stitching that traps our self-sabotage. It allows us to peel away the old cloths that cover our bodies so we may look within and heal.

I close my eyes and visualize my grandfather before me. I blink them open after a few seconds, still not fully capable of staring at him, at his memory. A few deep breaths later, I blink my eyes shut again and visualize his face before I begin to speak in my mind.

Why, why, why? Why couldn't you be the person you pretended to be? Or at the very least, be honest. I'd prefer an asshole of a grandfather than a deceitful one. You ruined so much.

My inhale is strong as it vibrates up my body, the sadness remaining on the shore. I must stop the judgment.

I don't need to pretend to be strong.

Slowly, I blink my eyes, willing the trapped tears to move freely. Soft pain trails my cheeks as the sorrow of a little girl breaks free. My body trembles with the cries, silent and all-consuming, wracking my body front and back. *Release.*

Something Makenna told me moves to the front of my mind, as I remember her sad smile as she spoke. *"You don't need to be completely healed to be loved and love. Being in a relationship with someone, a partnership, is part of the healing, therefore, how can we fully heal if we think we're not good enough for a person? They are a part of our path for that purpose. Maybe with this experience, part of your healing is accepting you are good enough to be loved unconditionally for who you are, good for more than physical contact. You don't need to give so much of yourself without receiving in return. It's all about balance. Give yourself permission to receive love and care and someone else's heart."*

Experiences mark us, I've learned this firsthand, but we have the power over our own lives. I've been living with this guilt, with this anger, when I have the choice to release it. It's just easier said than done. It's easier to romanticize healing than actually to live it. It's not as perfect and smooth as it's expressed. Healing is messy and painful, but once we do, we come out freer and lighter.

Matthias. I close my eyes and see his smirk sketched on his face. His bright eyes and wavy hair free as he watches me. My chest constricts as I remember his sad smile yesterday as he hopped into his car. When it comes to us, time is an illusion, but I'll be damned if it doesn't feel like an eternity since I felt his arms hold me tight in the middle of the night and his warm breath melt the ice around me.

We were born from the same star.

We were supposed to meet. I let Matthias leave because I was scared of what staying would mean. I allowed my fear rule me, and I let my analytical judgment control what was right and wrong as if such a thing exists. Because of my own pain, I've been so miserable and numb that I haven't supported him. *Selfish*. I deliberately lost my way.

Who cares if I still can't face my grandfather? I'm working on it. I need to be easier on myself, more understanding. I embrace the truths I carry because they're mine, they're a part of my path, but I don't need to let it define me. I can take them as my lessons so I can grow, but ultimately I'm more than the shame, than the pain. I embrace the little girl and move forward with her sans scars. Souls can't be punctured, only love can fill them. It's the only thing that truly exists. It's what the universe is made of, and it heals all. Love isn't a lie.

Oh, my God.

My heart races as I run into my room and throw on sneakers and a sweatshirt. I grab my phone and keys, locking up my apartment and jogging down the stairs. Once outside, I look right and left before heading toward the right, speed-walking.

I'm wild and erratic as I take the route I barely remember, paying close attention to similar landmarks and street names, swirling through the roads.

I look around my surroundings, the sun already set, and wipe my face with the sleeve of my sweater.

Love is a truth.

Love is a truth.

Love is a truth.

I race faster in my search for the cottage in the countryside. The further away I get from the town center the darker the streets become. I turn on the flashlight on my phone and hope my battery holds off until I arrive.

Shining the light on the street name, I try to jog my memory. If only I had paid more attention when coming this way. I continue in the direction that feels right just as my phone runs out of battery. I curse into the wind but squint my eyes and keep walking. His home is around here, I know it.

After a few minutes of breathing quickly and being ultra-aware of every detail I can make out under the dark sky, I see the familiar home tucked away in the meadow.

I wipe my hands on my jeans although it's a pointless attempt. Only one light illuminates the inside, and I wonder how he'll react to seeing me here. I loosen my hair from the hair tie and redo my bun as best as I can.

Building courage, I walk up to the wooden door and knock. The door swings open and wide eyes meet my uncertain ones before a smile sweeps across Matthias's face.

"Hello." He looks over my head to see behind me.

"Hi." I give a small wave and shake my head at my own awkwardness.

"Come in," Matthias invites me into his home, into his life.

I smile and walk in, instantly inhaling the scent of wood and spice. The flames from the fireplace draw me in as its warmth comforts me after walking around outside for a good half hour.

I shake my head when Matthias points to the couch, needing to stand as I speak. He remains standing as well. We're both silent, staring at each other—my hands tucked into the sleeves of my sweater, his in his jean pockets.

"Let me start by saying you were right. I was using a façade to protect myself because I've felt the need to be stronger for so long. You were right when you said I was hiding behind a mask of indifference and independence when in reality I just want you. It's what I've always wanted." I shrug, widening my eyes in an attempt to dry my tears enough that I can continue speaking.

"I've been waiting for you for so long I had an internal battle between you being too good to be true and excitement that you were in the flesh. I was afraid of what would happen, yet I couldn't stop myself from giving you my heart, because you already had it, from lifetimes long ago. But I've had people leave me in all ways, even not wanting to, and the little, disappointed girl reminded me of everything I had suppressed. The deaths I never mourned, the disappointments I never processed, the sadness I was still holding on to. I didn't want you to become one of those. If I lost you…" my voice cracks. I tuck my lips into my mouth, biting down on them.

Shaking my head, I say, "Losing you would feel as if I lost a piece of myself. We're separate people; however, our connection is so . . . I can't formulate my thoughts right now. I'm sorry." I turn around and pace, wiping my nose with the sleeve of my sweater and my face with the other one. Matthias gives me the time I need to regroup.

"I can't carry bullshit anymore. I'm so tired of it. I can't let other people's actions control me, have a power over me. I'm not responsible for them and what they did, I'm only responsible for myself. For so long, I allowed their actions to pave mine. When I was younger, I wasn't a good person. Or maybe I was, but I was so defensive, mean, I couldn't see the good in me. So many times I feel the need to punish myself instead of celebrating where I've gotten in life. I'm all sorts of messed up, and although I've really shifted in the last few years, I'm still learning.

"The only difference is I now have tools to work through my fears, anxiety, negative thoughts. I'm still human though, and I'm going to mess up. I'm going to push at times, but I'll also pull. I've been stuck in my own emotions after they stirred up that I didn't even think to support you.

It was selfish of me. You also have your own experiences to sort through, and I wasn't there for you. Instead, I let you walk away. I watched you leave and remained silent when I should've called out that I never wanted you to go. I never wanted to hurt you like that. I never wanted to make you walk. I'm sorry." I stop pacing and look up at Matthias. My throat burns as I wait for him to speak.

"There's nothing to apologize for." He shakes his head when I open my mouth, so I clamp it shut. "It's what we needed. Did it help you work through your issues?" I nod. "Me, too. I was able to really look at myself and realize I was also carrying a lot of hatred. I spoke to my parents and told them what happened to me when I was a child. It was good. I thank you for that courage. You may not see it, but you pushed me to break away from my own hiding places. One day I may be the one to push. The important thing is that one of us pulls, that we grow and communicate. You needed space. I said things that maybe were too harsh. The one thing I can promise is that you'll never lose me. Our connection is far too deep, too ingrained into our true existence, to lose one another. This experience in this physical life is just one of many." He walks to me, his hand cradling my face.

"We've got a ways to go." He reaches for my hand with his other one and squeezes. "But I promise to walk it together, hand in hand."

"I promise, too."

"Good because I want to kiss you now." His lips descend on mine, brushing once, twice, before I open my mouth and invite him in. My tongue sweeps against his, and I sigh, feeling immense emotions as we reunite. My arms reach around his neck and hold on tight as our lips mold together. It's slow and gentle, both of us taking our time to reconnect in all ways.

"I've missed you," Matthias confesses as our lips part. "I also have."

"No more apologizing," he reads my mind. "We needed that." He guides us to the sofa, sitting and bringing me onto his lap. "Tell me what you've done."

So I do. I tell him about my talks with Makenna, my own writing, and the realizations I've had these last couple weeks.

"Love is a truth," he repeats after me. "I like that."

"You taught me that," I pinch my lips as a smile sneaks its way on my mouth.

"I love you, Navia." He brushes his lips against mine.

I nod and grin. "I love you, too." I say it without any preconceived ideas of what love should be and just feel it.

"Stay the night," he asks.

"Unless you drive me home, I intend to stay."

"Did you walk here?" He shifts us, so we're lying on the sofa.

"Yes," I nod for emphasis.

"You're insane," he chuckles. "It's not around the corner."

"I needed to see you. I needed to talk to you. As soon as it dawned on me that the only truth in life is love, I ran out and walked this way." Love is the healing force. When we fill ourselves with it, the vacancies we feel are no longer.

"You could've called me." He shifts his body, so he's holding me but still looking at my face.

"I didn't think about it. Maybe I wanted the element of surprise?" I shrug as much as I can.

"You surprised me, all right. I'm glad you did." He kisses my forehead. "I've thought about reaching out, but I didn't want to interfere if you weren't ready to see me."

I nod. "I'd always be ready to see you, but I understand what you're saying. I also realized that I can't punish the ghost of my grandfather anymore. It only hurts me. He had his own role to play out in his life, as much as I may disagree with it. Maybe he did love us in his own, twisted way. Maybe he loved us in the best way he could or knew how to. Maybe in his childhood, he was taught to only love conditionally. I don't know, but I can't hold on anymore. I don't think I'll ever be okay with him. A part of me will always be angry. But I've chosen not to hold on to it." It isn't mine to own; therefore, I send it off to the wind like the petals of a dandelion, carrying away my wishes.

"That's a brave choice. You can forgive a little each day. No one said you have to be okay with every hurt. It's the harboring it that is damaging. The judgment of others we don't truly know about that scrapes us."

We continue to talk, Matthias holding me as we move to the floor, closer to the fireplace. This is happiness. I feel free after expressing everything to him. I feel free after realizing I don't need to take on other people's baggage. It's not my responsibility.

19
soul beings

I step out of the cabin, rested and refreshed. What a difference a full night's sleep makes. Matthias brought me here last night after spending the day together in his cottage, reconnecting in more ways than just words. When we arrived here last night, I was exhausted, slumber conquered me like a wildfire in a dry forest. Now, I stare out onto the meadow, breathing in the fresh air as the sun rises in the sky. I've been here for a couple of months, and I'm still captivated by the town and people who live here.

The small flowers dance in the breeze, and I sit on the steps of the front porch and watch them sway, my breathing slowing down. My vision begins to blur, pulling me into meditation. I finally close my eyes and feel. I listen to the thumping in my chest and the rustling of nearby trees. The humid air swirls around me, and despite the cool weather, I feel my skin become damp with a fine layer of sweat. I inhale lavender, and the trickling sound of water fills my ears.

It would be nice to go see the river. Matthias mentioned it last night while we lay in front of the fireplace. He told me about this cabin, and the meaning it has to him, as he sipped whiskey and held me close. His attempt at being seductive only encouraged my sleep even more.

A smile washes over me as I remember. When I could no longer keep my eyes open, Matthias carried me to his bed and lay with me, making sure he never let go. I still managed to sneak out early to catch the sunrise. His sleeping face was the same as all the times I imagined him. All the times I knew he was there soulfully even if our bodies hadn't met yet.

"You snuck out on me." I smile as Matthias sits on the step above me, one leg on each side, and hugs me with love and protection.

"You know I love watching the sunrise."

"You do," he whispers in my ear, leaving a soft kiss right below it.

"I was meditating. This area is beautiful."

"Hmm . . . It is. Did I interrupt your meditation?"

"A little, but I'm glad you did. Do you ever wonder how people levitate while meditating?"

He chuckles. "I've thought about it, but I don't put my energy into it. Who knows?"

"Yeah." I nod against his chest.

"Do you want me to leave you alone a little longer?"

"No." I shake my head. "I just want to sit here and feel. Stay with me."

He tightens his arms around me. "I can do that."

I had a teacher once tell the me that using the term light warrior causes a negative vibration. She said to use words like worker or healer, but I like warrior. It reminds me of goddesses. I understand in part why she said it, but I think we give vibrations to words in how we use them. And although we aren't fighting like warriors, it's time for light to shine through us and protecting it like a warrior is brave and powerful.

Coming to live here was to fulfill that aspect of myself. The part of me that understands beyond this dimension and is prepared to help humanity.

"I have a surprise for later." His hands move up and down my arms.

"What is it?" I turn my head to look at him, his beard tickling my cheek.

"I can't tell you. It would ruin the surprise." His smirk is teasing.

"I don't like surprises," I mumble.

"You'll fancy this one." His eyes gleam under the rising sun, matching the sky above us.

"You're so sure," I tease, poking his shoulder.

"Positive."

I smile, shifting my body to look at him more clearly. I'm glad I decided to go to him, talk to him. My hands find his face, holding him just inches from me. "Thank you for bringing me here and telling me about this place."

"I'm glad I could share it with you, show you this part of me." He bought this cabin when he was younger with money he had saved, fixing it little by little. It was during his rebellious years when he wanted to break away from everything his family stood for because he knew there were other aspects of the world he hated. He opened up last night, and I listened, comforted him, and held him.

"Can we go to the river today?"

"Sure. The water will be ice cold, but it's beautiful nonetheless. Do you want coffee first?"

"Yes." I kiss his lips and stand, extending my hand to him. He takes it and stands, leading us into the house.

Matthias has been driving for a bit, and I still have no idea where we're going. He won't tell me, except that we have to be there by eight-thirty, and he's been staring at the time the entire drive over.

"Are we far?" I ask as I watch his jaw tick.

"We've got about another half hour."

"So we're doing good on time," I point out, noticing it's

seven forty-five.

He nods, focusing on the road. I admire the vast land and hills as we continue on our drive. Every so often we drive by a home, but overall, it's empty fields, trees, and wildflowers. We follow the curves of the hills as he takes us further and further away from Glastonbury and closer to the surprise that has him swirling with nervous energy.

I sigh when we enter a part of the road that is shielded by abundant trees and green foliage. It's like being transported through a portal, the trees adding magic to the journey.

I suddenly sit taller, staring out the window and then back at Matthias, who is looking at me out of the corner of his eye. Heart racing, I fight my emotions as I crane my neck to look ahead for a sign that he's really bringing me here.

I receive the confirmation when Matthias pulls into the parking lot for Stonehenge.

"I don't even know what to say." I look at him as he turns off the ignition.

"You say nothing. Just feel." He grasps my hand and squeezes before opening the door and stepping out. I'm out of the car before he even has a chance to make his way around, and chuckles at my reaction. The area is empty as we walk, hand in hand, toward a staff member. Matthias shows him our tickets and shares we're here for the sunset tour. I look up at him with pinched eyebrows as I listen to him speak.

"We'll be ready to begin in about twenty minutes. You're welcome to wait by the roped path and begin your visit there," the tour guide tells us.

"Thank you," Matthias smiles and leads me toward the stone I've only ever dreamt about visiting. I stare in awe the closer we get, trying to imagine how life was back then when this was a complete and populated area.

"How did you even get tickets? Don't you need to book months in advance? And a private tour?" I look at him with wide eyes, almost with as much awe as the stone before me.

He chuckles and keeps his hold on my hand. "I'm a member of the National Trust. I guess I got lucky they had an opening today. I'll blame the recent rain and people thinking it wouldn't be good weather to enjoy the sunset."

"Thank you," I whisper. "This is beautiful. Are we really going to walk up to the stone?"

"We are." Matthias moves to drape an arm around my shoulders and pulls me to him. Kissing the top of my head, he says, "Isn't it amazing?"

"Yes," I sigh. I never would've imagined this would be his surprise. He was right, this is one surprise I love. When it's closer to the sunset, the tour guide comes to us and begins to lead us beyond the rope that keeps tourists separate from the giant stones. The closer we get, the more peace I feel. We're silent as we admire the area. Matthias has been here before, but I still notice his silent and reflective demeanor.

The history that fills this space is magical. No one truly knows how this was built or the real purpose, but theories can be drawn up. Maybe some people do know and keep it hidden, so the sacredness of the space remains despite the tourists that visit yearly.

We each go our separate ways. I move through the stones, inhaling the clear air and closing my eyes. I place my hands over my heart and silently thank the Universe for bringing me here, for allowing me to have the courage to take a leap of faith.

"What do you think?" Matthias meets me.

"It's amazing."

"The sun is setting." We stand on the outside of the circle and watch as the sun descends. Soothing emotions enter as I take in the scenery around me, the remote space filled with such amazing history. For someone who loves history, this is a dream, and I absorb it through the pores of my skin so it can settle in my soul. A little piece of me is amongst these rocks, and I reclaim it. I reclaim the part of me that is older and wiser than this life. I shake off the dust of uncertainty and fear so that what is left of me is ancient wisdom combined with present experiences and infinite magic.

As the sun hides in the horizon, specs of light pop up in the sky. Stars that remind me of the infinite expansion the universe offers us, of lives before this one, and how Matthias and I are tied to the very beginning of our being.

I lie down on the damp grass and stare up at the sky amongst this prehistoric site. More and more stars show themselves as the sky darkens. They're galaxies away, and I wonder what life is like out there.

Matthias's hand inches toward mine, his fingers grazing my skin as I shiver. He left enough space between us when he joined me on the ground, but we will always find each other despite the distance.

I turn my head toward him. Feeling my gaze on him, he turns to look at me. "I want you to visit Spain with me."

A slow smile creeps across his lips. "I'd love that."

My smile mirrors his and I nod before fully reaching for his hand and tangling our fingers. My skin tingles at our union.

When we've stared at the stars and danced with the energy of the generations that came before us, the people who first lived this land, we leave.

"Thank you." I kiss Matthias on the cheek as he drives us back to Glastonbury, the fields I admired on the way here now dark blurs as he takes us home.

20

fairies & magic

I grip the handle on the inside of the rental we picked up at the airport when we landed. Matthias is driving us away from the city and into the countryside despite my parents insisting they pick us up. I wanted to have some mobility while we're here and not put my parents out without a car if we borrowed theirs.

"Are you used to driving on this side of the road and car?" I tease Matthias in an attempt to calm my nerves.

He chuckles and shakes his head. "It's quite odd but not impossible to get accustomed to."

"Good because I can't string stick shift, so we'd never make it if I had to drive."

"I could teach you," he offers.

"I think the time for me to learn passed. Not sure I have the patience to learn now."

"You do. You can even learn to drive in the UK on the 'wrong' side of the road," his smile is wide.

I shrug and look out the window. "God, I love the mountains." I admire the huge humps that grow from the earth and overpower every other view. For me, there is nothing more beautiful as the magic of mountains.

"It's beautiful," Matthias agrees.

We enter the road that leads to my dad's village, eucalyptus and pine trees creating an arch in the sky so we drive through a tunnel of pure nature.

"This is my dad's favorite part of the drive," I share

with Matthias.

"I can't wait to meet him." My hand grips the door handle again, and I tense. "Don't be nervous," he comforts.

"It's weird. I mean, I asked you to come so obviously I wanted you to, but I don't know, it has been a *long*"—my eyes widen—"time since I've introduced my parents to a man. Let alone someone like you, someone with a connection like ours. It has nothing to do with whether or not you'll like each other. It has everything to do with showing others a part of me that's vulnerable, it's like another mask I remove. I'm so used to pretending I don't need this"—I motion between us—"and that I'm not the type to open to someone else, be this soft and gentle person because I've had to be strong for so long," I continue to ramble, though it oddly makes sense. If he can follow along with my word vomit, I'd be impressed. Of course, he can, though. I'm sure he reads me before I open my mouth to speak.

"Navia," he breathes out my name in a way that washes over my skin. "Breathe, love. You don't have to pretend, especially with your family. Less so with me."

I nod, trapping my breath in my lungs like a warden determined to keep the criminals locked up for an eternity.

"Breathe," he reminds me. I slowly exhale through my mouth as I signal the left turn into the village.

"I feel like I should warn you."

"Stop. No warnings, no worries. Let me experience this. I will make my own opinions and enjoy my visit."

"Okay." I nod once, biting the inside of my lower lip. So many things crowd my mind about my family here, but I let it go with the wind.

We drive into the village, and I point out my parents' house to the left as soon as we enter. I take a moment to admire the town laid out in front of me from this point above on the hill. As the hill before us dips, the houses emerge, providing a view of dwellings and mountains that bring a sense of peace and home.

Matthias parks across in the driveway and exits the car, as he stares up at the gray sky. "You were right, this weather is quite similar to ours."

"Yeah."

Then, he looks up at the two-story house and across the street where the stream travels lazily. "It's beautiful." He makes his way to the trunk to remove our bags.

"I'll take you around for a tour after." I grab his hand, my bag in my other one, and lead him up the stairs, where of course, my mom is already opening the door.

Her smile is wide as she greets us.

"Hi, Mom. This is Matthias."

"Hi, I'm Lily," my mom interrupts me in her excitement.

"Well, there you go." I shake my head in amusement.

"It's very nice to meet you," Matthias tells her, his British accent more pronounced against my mom's Spanish one.

"Come in. How was your flight?" We walk in, my dad in the living room with the television on, but I'm sure he's aware of our entrance and conversation.

"Good. It was smooth," I tell her as I go say hi to my dad.

"Hello, my dear." I smile and hug him when he stands. His attention turns to Matthias. "Hello, young man. I'm Diego."

"I'm Matthias. So nice to meet you," they shake hands.

We sit in the living room, watching my parents interact with Matthias without missing a beat. The last time my parents met a boyfriend I was eighteen. It's been quite a few years since then, and I'm a different person. Matthias is an entirely different person than him. My parents and I have a different relationship than we did back then.

"Do you want anything to eat or drink?" My mom looks at us both.

"I wanted to show Matthias around a little before the sun sets."

"Go ahead. When you come back, we'll have happy hour and then go out for dinner," my dad nods. I smile at my parents, feeling as if I'm having an out of body experience, and lead Matthias to my bedroom to drop off our bags.

He looks at the space, not much decor but just enough to show him another piece of me. He finds old photographs from my teen years, smiling as he stares at them. "I didn't know you had braces."

I shrug. "It never came up."

"These were your friends?" His chin juts toward the pictures in small frames adorned with rhinestone borders. They're so tacky now, but when I was fifteen, they were all that.

"Yeah. That was when I was middle school and high school. It's been a few years," I tease.

"I like seeing the different phases of your life." He walks to me, holding my hips. "I like seeing the place you're so fond of." His lips touch mine in a brief and electrifying kiss. Having him here is something I couldn't even imagine. I could feel him, connect with him, but we never got this far. I never showed him all of me when I would dream of him.

"Are you ready?" I keep my hold around his waist.

"Lead the way." His hand seeks mine. I never want to let go. It's impossible. Even if I *did* want to, I wouldn't be capable of it. Matthias and I have been tied for eons. Even in our attempt to give each other space to work through our baggage, we were connected.

I make a right as we walk out of the driveway and onto the street. "We're going to go to a hidden river where we used to swim when we were kids. I don't know if the trees are too overgrown to go all the way down, but it's worth a shot."

"Take me everywhere you want. I'm yours." He squeezes my fingers.

We follow the road that lines the property of my parents' house and my aunt's house, both sharing space on the same land. I turn around, extending our arms and walking backward so I can face Matthias.

"In the summers, blackberries grow on these shrubs. Anytime I'm visiting in summer, I pick blackberries and eat them. They're my favorite, and there's something magical about eating fruit that grows wild. It reminds me we're all wild in our core. I've also always admired how a plant with such treacherous thorns could produce such delicious fruit. Not everything is as it seems, and even something that appears to be harmful can be beneficial."

I look at the plants growing from the mountainside and smirk. Pointing to small flowers, I show Matthias the proof. He listens with a smile, silent as he observes his surroundings. We continue our trek, rounding the land until we begin to enter the wooded area of town. I inhale eucalyptus, its soothing scent calming my nerves and mind.

"This is beautiful," Matthias comments.

I nod, taking it in. Giant pines surround us on either side of the elevated land as we walk on the path carved between the mountains. No matter the years, this has always felt like home.

Matthias chuckles when I swing our connected arms between us, my free arm up in the air. I've always felt free here. Nature, me, and the energy.

We walk in silence, pausing every so often to admire a rock or mushroom growing from the earth. Following the path, I have engraved in my memory, we make our way to the opening that leads to the river. The swooshing sound resonates around us as the river below rushes and sprints through boulders.

The uneven path that leads down to the riverbed is overgrown with plants, but we can step through them. "Are you okay walking down through this?" I look back at Matthias over my shoulder.

"Let's do it." He claps his hands. His body is humming with excitement and curiosity.

We begin our descent, careful not to slip on the damp soil, as the sound of water becomes louder. With a final leap, we land on the riverbed, and I pause to take it in. The area is unkempt, but I didn't expect any different. This is nature, a creation of the Earth, not a vacation spot. That is what I love so much about it.

"I've always wanted my ashes spread here when I die." I break our silence and through the sound of birds chirping and the water spilling over the small waterfall.

"How come?" Matthias looks at me intently.

"I've always felt a connection with this area. Something about it."

"If I'm still alive by the time you're gone, I promise to come to this very spot and fulfill your wishes."

My heart skids to a stop. I blink my eyes and frown. "I don't like to think about that. While I know our bodies and this world will fade into oblivion at one point, in my mind, right now, the thought of a life without feeling you is suffocating."

He hugs me to his chest, holding me gently. With a kiss to the crown of my head, he says, "You'll always feel me deep in your soul. No matter where we are in our existence, we will be together. Besides, we've got a whole life together to enjoy." He leans back and smirks. Keeping a hold on my hand, he explores the area. I tell him about our summers here with my cousins, bringing a picnic and pretending we were experts exploring the way the river traveled and the purpose it had for people in ancient times. We would splash and play games and feel invincible despite the freezing water and the waterfall just feet away. It all swirled into a magical experience where the world as I knew it ceased to exist and all that mattered was the power of trees, the cleansing water, and the freshest air my lungs had ever swallowed.

21
sacred union

I've missed this place, the air and the direction the wind blows. I've missed the mountains the most, and I feel blessed to be able to visit. I feel fortunate to have brought Matthias here. The last two days have been amazing, and I've merged the me he knows to a part of me I keep very private.

"Ready?" I look at him as we stand at the base of a hill.

"Yes."

We begin climbing the pebbled path that leads to one of my favorite places. A chapel I've never entered rises on the right, at the top of the hill. To the left is part of the site we came to admire. Matthias looks around in silence. As we reach the top and round the chapel, I stare out at the view in front of me. Mountains, clouds, and sun. Nothing else but nature's beauty, the Earth's energy, and us.

I lead Matthias further into this piece of land until I see the circular homes.

"Wow." I watch him move his gaze from stone home to stone home, all in ruins of what's left of them, but their history dug so deep into it that it will never be uprooted.

"It's amazing, right? It's not a big Celtic site, but I connected to it so deeply the first time I came." I walk down the few steps that give me better access to be amongst the piled stones that create the place that kept the people here safe from weather and invaders. I graze one of the stones with my fingers, spinning around slowly to get a full view. Matthias is smiling, still at the top of the steps.

"You love it here," he states, knowingly. I nod and smile.

"I don't know what it is about it. I could spend hours here, just listening to the wind as it whispers truths I've been seeking my whole life. The first time I came here, I walked around, took tons of pictures, and felt. The second time, I sat in silence on those stones"—I point to the home to my right, near where Matthias is standing—"and listened. My feet dangled into the house, and the sun illuminated every inch." I turn around, my back to Matthias, and stare off the edge of the mountain, peeks of other mountains popping up amongst the low-hanging clouds.

I sense his footsteps as he stands behind me. His arms wrap around my shoulders, his hands resting over my chest. "A long time ago we lived in a similar setting together." It's a simple phrase that holds the key to who we are, separate and together.

"Yes," I affirm although he doesn't ask. "I've seen bits of that." I lean back, allowing him to hold me. With Matthias, I've learned it's okay to be supported and still stand on my own two feet. What I believed was a weakness was, in fact, strength because alone we can only do so much, but with the support and love of the right people, we can accomplish miracles. This, he and I, standing together only multiplies our purpose, not diminishes it. We don't have to let go of a part of ourselves to feed someone else's purpose. With a balance of giving and taking, we feed our own while supporting the other's. We grow and fortify.

Matthias and I walk through the site, imagining life here before the people were forced to move on. We talk about the homes and what we know about the lifestyle. After we finish exploring this part, we return to the top of the path that led us here, and explore the other side, with more homes built on the edge of the mountain. The way they lived is amazing—their wisdom is still present today. After thousands of years, their homes are standing, albeit not fully, but powerful in their structures. If we could take a lesson from this, it is that a community builds a stronger foundation than a competition to outgrow your neighbor.

"Are you ready to leave tomorrow?" Matthias glances at me as we walk back to the car.

"Yeah."

"Are you sure? Would you like to live here someday?" He tilts his head, his hand holding me from continuing my feet from moving forward. I halt and look at him with furrowed brows.

I shake my head. "No. Not anytime soon at least. I can't say what I'll feel in the future, but right now I belong in England. It's my *home*."

"Would you run away without me?" His usually soft features are tense.

"No more running."

"But would you?" His vulnerability shows as he runs his free hand through his waves.

"I'd stay where you are. Life wouldn't be an adventure without you."

"Some days I feel like you'll expand to the point where you'll need something greater than I can offer you." I smooth his eyebrows with my thumbs until the skin around his eyes relaxes.

"All I've ever searched for, even when I rejected the idea of it, was you." I cup his face. "You taught me that not everyone leaves. It was silly of me to think that I'd have everything figured out by the time I met you. I'd be in this 'perfect' place in my life that we would fall into step seamlessly and love fiercely without pain. Meeting you was humbling. It proved to me that my healing process is lifelong, in different phases, but I don't need to be perfect for you. I don't need to be perfect for anyone. Perfection is an illusion we hide behind, so others don't see our flaws. My flaws are printed on my skin, and I decided some time ago it wasn't my job to hide them. I'd never be able to help others heal if I covered my scars.

"You know what I love most? That you don't hide yours anymore either. You not only embrace my imperfections because you love me, but you also embrace yours because you love yourself. So no, I'll never run. You have everything and more to offer than you can even imagine. We're constantly changing, like the phases of the moon, so we expand together." I raise on my toes and touch my lips to his.

Matthias's hands instantly go to my waist, holding me to him, as my hands slip from his face to the back of his neck. My fingers tangle in the curls on the back of his head as my tongue seeks his. My body hums and tingles at the feel of his mouth on mine and his hands squeezing my sides. Heart racing, the feeling of kissing Matthias carries me away as if I were weightless. The intimacy of our contact sneaks into my bones and vibrates in my cells. With eyes closed, I feel dizzy, as if I'm spinning with him, our bodies twirling to the rhythm of our kiss.

Matthias slows our movements, kissing me twice straight on the lips before moving his head a few inches away. "Marry me."

My racing heart stops on cue. My breath gets trapped in my lungs. My head spins faster than when we were kissing. "What?" I blink a few times and stare at his eyes, searching for something more than the two words he just spoke.

"Marry me." There's no mistake in what he said. His

eyes are smiling despite his teeth biting his lips. Marriage? We never talked about that. We only just met, technically. *What if…*

"Is it crazy to say yes?" I surprise the both of us with my response.

Matthias chuckles. "You're asking the man who just proposed. I'm mad with you."

"Is it too soon?" I speak my fear.

"It's been too long," Matthias contradicts. I nod and smile. Way too long. Now that he's here, it feels like we've been apart for too long.

"Okay. Yes. Wow." My eyes water as the significance of this moment plays out in slow motion.

When I realize he's reaching into his pocket, the tears fall faster. My vision is blurred as he opens the box and I see three rings. My eyes snap to his. Matthias is wearing a gentle smile and intense eyes.

"I bought this the day you saw me across the street, climbing into my car. I know we needed our space, and it was so easy to chase you, but I tried not to. Instead, I found this perfect symbol of my love for you, so I bought it. All the stones are sapphire, even the orange. Today, I'll only give you the center ring, the other two bands are for our wedding." I watch him slip off a ring that has a gold circle with ridges and a round, orange sapphire in the center of the circle.

"This is my promise to always chase the stars with you and rest in the forests with the fairies beside you." The cold metal tickles my skin as he slips the ring on my finger.

"What do the other two rings symbolize?" My eyes haven't left his.

"You and me. The cool, blue band is your feminine beauty and nurturing nature. The orange band is for me. My promise to always keep your days bright and illuminated, support you and your wisdom, and share my own warmth with you."

"Yin and yang," more tears fall.

"Yes. Both of our counterparts coming together to form a whole while remaining true to ourselves." I stare at the two bands that curve to frame the one on my finger. Each one with small, round sapphires framing it, reminding me of the sun and moon.

I kiss him again, this time slow and sensual. I push my body to his, needing to feel him. It's too much, what I feel for him. I only ever thought this kind of love existed for the rare fortunate ones to find it. A privilege many times I didn't think I deserved.

"I love you," I whisper against his lips.

"I love you, too." I shiver upon hearing his words, the sky growing with clouds. "Are you cold?"

"No. I can't explain what I feel, but it's not cold."

Matthias nods with a smile. "It's our destiny."

I've spent a lot of my life questioning the cards I've been dealt. I've spent years confused as to how and why things happen. I've denied people I used to love. I've turned my back on those I cared about because it was easier than staying by their side as I watched them self-destruct. I've set the timer on my own bomb. I've walked crooked paths, made unethical choices, broken the law and a few hearts. I've deemed myself unworthy of love, convinced myself affection was war, and that pain was peace. My hurt was multiplied the further I walked in life because it fed a part of me that thrived on it. I've judged and convicted sinners when my own sins were dangling next to theirs. I've turned a blind eye when I should've been present and brave enough to make a stance.

I have imperfections. I have weapons that can destroy others. I've used some of them to destroy myself. I've played with fire and danced in the smoke.

I've been a wild child and imprisoned adult.

The one thing I've never done is allow my heart to be open, to welcome love like this. I've never given myself permission to surrender to all my desires. Some people wear rose-colored glasses. I owned filth-colored ones.

But now I've removed it all. The judgments, pain, anger, disgust, shame. I stand before a man, willing to make an eternal life with him because I've dealt with myself. I've listened to what I had to say because how can we expect others to hear when we ignore ourselves?

It's time I live out my destiny without the bullshit baggage.

I close my eyes and send it all to the wind, in this sacred space, until I am weightless. No longer a feeling, but a state. Wings like fairies to fly with and shine in my eyes like stars that illuminate millions of miles away.

I hold Matthias's hand with both of mine and smile. "Let's save this moment." I get my phone from my back pocket and hold my arm out to take a picture of us. I smile and snap three photos.

Turning my phone around to look at them, I see the first of us both smiling at the camera. The other two Matthias is looking at me. Seeing the way he looks at me, I breathe out lightly and know that time doesn't matter. It's not too soon or too long. Us, here, is perfect timing.

22
pink skies & lullabies

I roll out of bed as stiffly as I can and tiptoe out of the room and out the patio doors. *Perfect timing.* I stand in the chill of the early morning and cross my arms. I'm tempted to run in for a jacket but don't want to miss the sunrise. I still get surprised by the cool air when we're already in summer. The weather here is different from where I came from, no heatwave or suffocating humidity. I smile as I can now think back to my birthplace with peace.

Through the leaves of the oak tree, I see the rays of the sun peeking. My arms fall to my sides as I stare in awe of the majestic sun rising. After last night's raging thunderstorm, I was unsure if the sky would be clear this morning. The lingering smell of hay from the humidity is the only proof that it rained yesterday.

My skin pebbles as I close my eyes and breathe deeply. Gratitude fills me as the bright light dances through my eyelids. I follow the light, watching it intensify and diminish behind my lids.

I open my eyes with a start and look to the right, sensing movement. A small smile covers my face. I'm not used to this, not accustomed to sharing my space with someone. Yet here he is. Here we are.

As soon as we returned from Spain two months ago, I moved into Matthias's cottage. Living further away from the city has been a dream, but Matthias has still been unsuccessful in teaching me to drive. I smile at the memory of the last time he gave me a lesson.

"I wanted to watch the sunrise," I state.

"I figured." His eyes smile as I take in his mussed hair and bare chest. "Can I join you?"

One of my favorite things about him is that he asks for permission. He understands the sacredness of time to myself. He understands me. I nod, looking back at the sun. Above the branches now, its light shines with more intensity.

Matthias stands behind me. He doesn't touch my skin, but his presence surrounds me nonetheless. Front to back, we stand in silence below the rising day as the poetry of life makes verses of our love.

His energy resonates with mine, every day connecting deeper and more profoundly. When I shiver, he wraps his arms around me, holding me to him. Being with him like this is like foreplay for my soul.

"You shouldn't be out here without a sweater," he chastises, his palms sneaking under my shirt and pressing against my stomach.

I shiver against his cold hands. "I've only been here a few minutes."

"Let's go inside," he whispers into my ear, my skin tingling for a different reason now. I place my hands on his forearms, my wedding rings catching my attention. The orange stone warms me, just like the sky as the sun rises. We didn't wait longer than a month to get married.

It was just Matthias and me in the forest by the cottage with a minister. We exchanged promises to love fiercely and support each other every day. It was simple, intimate, and ours. Matthias in black pants and a white dress shirt with the first two buttons undone. I wore a flowing, blush pink dress and flowers in my hair.

We spent that night eating under the starry sky and

laughing.

Matthias had arranged for my parents to visit a couple of days after, so we had dinner with his family, mine, and Makenna. I couldn't have asked for a better celebration.

"Come on." He tugs my hand and walks us back into our home. Gently, Matthias sits me on top of the table in the center of the kitchen and hands me a bowl of cherries.

"Eat while I make tea," he pecks my lips. My stomach growls, causing me to giggle.

"My brother arrives next Tuesday," I remind him. "I've already told Makenna I won't be seeing clients that day."

He nods. "We'll drive to Bristol to pick them up." Matthias hands me a hot mug with a steeping teabag. My brother, Marcos, and my sister-in-law, Becky, are coming to visit. They were the only ones missing from our ceremony, but I'm happy Matthias will meet them soon. We have a more unconventional relationship than they do, and although they haven't said as much, I know they are anxious to meet Matthias. I can imagine their thoughts about my meeting him and being married within a few months. It's insane when I think about it from a disconnected point of view, however, waiting even longer would've been a waste of time.

"Thank you." I lean forward and pucker my lips, asking for a kiss. Matthias chuckles and obliges. .He taps the top of my thigh, and I climb down, sitting at the breakfast table with him.

"You're gonna spoil me with this kind of breakfast." My stomach growls as I look at the fried eggs, sausage, and toast.

"I gotta keep you fed and healthy," he winks. "You are cooking our baby." The joy that surrounds him melts away my fears of being pregnant, of bringing a baby into this world, of being a mother. All of it melts away when I see his smile and the way his eyes shine.

I had no idea I was pregnant when we flew to Spain. It would've been too soon to know anything, but it somehow happened. Something doctors throughout the years assured me would take time and patience to achieve because of my health challenges. I guess when the Universe has a plan for you, nothing stands in the way.

I remember taking the test a couple weeks ago. I'm not even sure why I bought it. My body is so irregular I never know if I'm starting my menstrual cycle or finishing it. Yet, I bought a pregnancy test and took it while Matthias sat in the living room, oblivious to my plan. I waited, heart in my throat and palms sweaty until the results came in. Then, I took the second one, just in case. Both positive.

I almost threw up. Then, I cradled my stomach and cried. Tears of joy mixed with tears of sadness. I wasn't sure what to feel.

For so long I never wanted to be a mother. I never wanted to bring a human into this world where shit was so fucked up. And that was before I knew everything my family had lived through.

Years ago, I had a vision, a meditation, almost as if I had split into two places at once. I was at home, in the kitchen, talking to my mom and my aunt, but all I saw was me coming home from work and walking through a dimly lit house. It was my home, but not the same I was currently standing in. I moved with ease, with only one destination in mind. As soon as I arrived, I leaned against the doorframe and saw a man holding our tiny daughter, humming to her so softly. I had never experienced unconditional love before that moment.

I got a tiny taste of it before it was ripped from me,

back to the present where I stood in a kitchen where there was no man and no baby. Freaking out, I ran to the bathroom and then prayed for that reality. I suddenly had an urge to have a child, to be a partner to someone. I wanted that more than my stubborn independence.

Since then, I'd had dreams. Dreams with a little girl, eyes so blue and a smile so soft. A delicate being that was mine to protect. I'd have other dreams with a man I knew from the moment I met him. But I never again had the same vision with both in one.

Now, it's as if both parallel universes crashed and created their own.

When I finally stopped the crying, I walked up to Matthias with the pregnancy test in my hand. He looked up at me from the book he was reading on the couch. Wordlessly, I handed him the test. When he realized what I was communicating, he tossed the book to a side and pulled me to him. Standing between his legs, he lifted my shirt and began kissing my belly like a maniac in love. I guess that's what he is.

Some moments I forget I'm pregnant, like this morning when I carelessly walked out into the cold with nothing but a thin tee shirt and pajama shorts. It hits me suddenly. Usually when I catch Matthias looking at me when he thinks I'm deep in thought. Other days, I wake up with my hand already placed on my stomach, wondering when I'll be showing.

We've agreed not to tell anyone until I'm further along, and we were worried about flying so early on, but the doctor assured us everything was okay.

"Eat," Matthias demands. I smirk and continue eating my breakfast. Although we have no idea if we're having a boy or girl yet, Matthias swears it's the same little girl with blue eyes.

Secretly, I'm hoping she is.

～

"To Navia," Matthias raises his glass, and everyone follows. I lift my water and playfully roll my eyes. There's nothing I hate more than attention. "I'm proud of you and your success." Everyone else cheers in agreement and clinks their glasses together.

We're gathered with Matthias's friends, who have become close to me, and my Marcos and Becky. *The Keeper of Secrets* was picked up by my first choice publisher, and we've quickly begun working together. The process is different than publishing fiction, but I've learned so much, starting with actually finishing a project I had given up on at one point. I thank Matthias for the completion of this, and I made that clear to him in my dedication.

I may not be one-hundred-perfect at peace with my grandfather, but I'm no longer so angry that I'm poisoning myself with his venom. Compassion has been the hardest lesson with him. I've started by having compassion for myself for still having some resentment, but I'm not clinging on to it. I want my baby to be born into a world where strength and love are maximized.

I take a moment just to observe our table, British and Americans laughing over drinks, asking what certain expressions mean despite the same language. I smile as my brother and James discuss the friendly rivalry between Real Madrid and Chelsea soccer teams.

He and Matthias hit it off. I could tell they were unsure of Matthias, but as soon as they sparked up a conversation on the drive back from the airport, I knew my brother approved. Becky gave me a thumbs up in the back seat on the way home. It's nice to have them here, celebrating a milestone and seeing where I live.

"Navia, you're one of us now. Tell your brother we've got the best teams in the world."

"Sorry, James. I'm a Real Madrid fan through and through," I shrug unapologetically.

"Bollocks," James calls out. "You married her, lad?" He looks at Matthias.

Laughing, Matthias places his arm around my shoulder. "And I'd do it a million times again." He kisses my cheek.

"Just don't convert to one of them," he smiles as he points at my brother and me.

"Never, a little friendly competition is healthy," Matthias responds and winks at me.

At the end of the evening, we return home. Marcos and Becky head to the guest bedroom, and Matthias and I stay on the couch for a bit, catching up on emails. He holds me close after I shut down my laptop, and I rest my head on his shoulder as his hand caresses my belly.

"I think Marcos and Becky are having a good time."

I nod against his shoulder. "They like you."

"I like them, too. It's a shame they live so far away," Matthias's breath tickles my cheek. "I guess we'll tell them the news once we're ready through video chat."

"Yeah, that would be nice." I shift closer to him, hugging his middle.

"We should name her Faye." My head snaps up, hitting his chin.

"Sorry!" I rub his face.

Matthias's laugh echoes. "That got your attention. I'm okay, love." He kisses my palm and moves me, so I'm sitting across his lap.

"You're so sure it's a girl."

"Ever since you told me about your dreams, I felt it was. Maybe not the exact same baby, but she was coming to you how you and I came together before we met." He wipes the tears that stream down my face.

"That would be sweet." I'm an emotional mess.

"I believe it's true. So what do you think? Faye?"

"It means fairy," I respond with a big smile.

"I know," he nods.

"I love it."

"I love you and that bean you're caring for." He kisses my lips, my cheeks, and my forehead.

When I moved here, I hoped for a story like ours. I never expected the pain that would come with it, the growth, and the healing. I expected a true fairytale, but we all know perfection like that doesn't even exist in movies. Matthias brought out the junk I had stored away, that I had thought I was done dealing with, and he allowed me the space to work it out. We both had to overcome things we didn't want to face, but we grew from it. He was right, we aren't like Sam and Max. Our purpose is different.

Our roles in each other's lives are bound by a timeless connection and a life together in this physical world.

This has allowed me to be a better guide for my clients in helping them heal. Matthias has helped me in a few group sessions, and it's been so amazing to work beside him and witness his wisdom. We make a pretty good team, partners in everything. The next romance I write will be ours, so the world knows that we don't need to have our shit together before we find a deep connection with someone else. That regardless of the crap, we deserve love. Our past doesn't own us. No one has everything together because we're continually digesting emotions and memories that may ignite pain. The real power is pushing through it. A butterfly's transformation causes discomfort and pain, but when its wings dry it's prepared for a new perspective.

I remember once Makenna asking me why I'd felt so lost in my life. I didn't want to tell her at first, but her words have stayed with me throughout this entire time. *"It's okay to feel lost and search for your soul. The pain you've endured is the same that has made you whole. Look in the mirror, and there you'll see that you're not lost at all. The same girl is still within."*

And she is, the same brave girl I remember from my childhood is still present within me. I'm still that person—wise, courageous, and kind. Now, I have the man that was created to be with me by my side. A man whose soul sparked with mine at the beginning of all things, destined to come together again when we were both ready. To work together for a greater good.

Publishing this book is the end of stigma. It led me back to that girl Makenna spoke about. Now my story will be out in the world without masks or pretenses. The truth laid bare as I move forward, prepared for where inspiration will lead me. With Matthias by my side, the embarrassment no longer exists. The pain is eased. The disgust dissipates. Forgiveness reigns.

I breathe deeply, exhaling the weight of the secrets I've held on to for so long, and feel Matthias's warmth surround me.

books by
fabiola francisco

Standalone

All My Truths & One Lie

Perfectly Imperfect

Red Lights, Black Hearts

Twisted in You

Memories of Us

Restoring Series

Restoring Us (Complete Series)

Resisting You (Aiden and Stacy Novella)

Sweet on You Series

Sweet on Wilde

Whiskey Nights

Rebel Desire Series

Lovin' on You

Love You Through It

All of You

acknowledgments

Let's me start by saying thank you to you, for picking up this book and taking the time to read my work. For your support and our belief in my words. Readers give life to authors' careers, and without you our art is for an empty audience. Thank you for your support, always.

Thank you to my family for supporting this crazy dream and encouraging me to keep going.

I'm blessed to have an amazing group of people that work with me throughout the entire process. Amy Queau, thank you for a gorgeous cover! Thank you for taking the time to make sure my "baby" is perfect. To Claire and Wendy from Bare Naked Words, who always make sure I have the best release and work hard to support me. Robin Bateman, I appreciate you and your hard work in editing my novel, Hurricane Florence and all. Cary Hart, thank you, thank you for making the inside of this book as stunning as the outside.

To Bex from Editing Ninja, I cannot thank you enough for making time to proofread this story and making sure I stay on schedule. I will *forever* be grateful for what you did.

Rach and Christy, God, what can I say? Soul sisters, soapy thighs for life, more than book friends. You two have been my rocks from the beginning and continue to be years later. Our friendship is rare, and I'd be lost without it.

Veronica and Miriam, I can never thank you enough for *always* reading my stories first, taking the time from your lives to give me feedback on my writing, and your unconditional support. I come back time and again with questions you're always willing to answer. Also, for making sure I put out what I write instead of rocking in a corner, hiding from the world.

Joy, I'm not sure how we went from meeting at a takeover a couple years ago and bonding over Brett Eldredge and boy bands to the friendship we have today, but I am *so* glad it happened. You always say I don't need to thank you, but I do. No matter the time, you're there for me, even with a seven hour time difference now. Thank you for working Happily Ever Insta and the hustle you put into supporting authors.

Brittany, you made sure to talk me off the ledge with this one. Many times. For that, I'll be forever grateful. Cary, thank you for being there. For checking in and listening when I needed someone to just hear me out. Ashley, our sprints keep me motivated. I'm so happy I have found people like you through this journey.

My Fab Readers, you are amazing! You keep me going each day, support me, encourage me. I love "hanging" out with you and sharing my work and life with you. You helped me write this book by offering your word prompts and feedback when I'd share the scenes with you. Because of you, this book is what it is. Thank you!

A huge thanks to my review team, who is always there to give feedback and answer questions. You all are amazing!

Authors and bloggers, coming together as a community always makes my heart happy. Thank you for your support, shares and laughs. It's amazing all the good we can do together. It feels great to belong to such a strong community.

about the
author

Fabiola Francisco loves the simplicity—and kick—of scotch on the rocks. She follows Hemingway's philosophy—write drunk, edit sober. She writes women's fiction and contemporary romance, dipping her pen into new adult and young adult. Her moods guide her writing, taking her anywhere from sassy and sexy romances to dark and emotion-filled love stories.

Writing has always been a part of her life, penning her own life struggles as a form of therapy through poetry. She still stays true to her first love, poems, while weaving longer stories with strong heroines and honest heroes. She aims to get readers thinking about life and love while experiencing her characters' journeys.

She is continuously creating stories as she daydreams. Her other loves are country music, exploring the outdoors, and reading.

Printed in Germany
by Amazon Distribution
GmbH, Leipzig